Thanks

Best Wishes !

An Uneaten Breakfast

Collected Stories and Poems

Joseph Anthony

Published by Diamond Mill Press

184 South Livingston Avenue, Suite 9-198

Livingston, NJ 07039

www.diamondmillpress.com

An Uneaten Breakfast

ISBN 978-0-9838745-9-1

Library of Congress Control Number: 2011937933

Cover art by Don Martinetti.

Cover design by Steven Seighman

Printed in the United States by Morris Publishing®
3212 East Highway 30
Kearney, NE 68847
1-800-650-7888

Dedicated to August J. Mauriello,

The grandfather I never had the privilege of knowing.

Acknowledgments

A profound thanks to Kelly Smith, without whom, none of this would be possible. Her mentorship and guidance have been invaluable and her patience has been a blessing. Endless thanks to Don Martinetti for the beautiful cover painting that draws people in and gives life to the work as a whole. His professionalism is only outdone by his talent as an artist. To my editors, Professor Susan Miller and Matthew Kosinski, whose diligence and efforts have helped turn this work into a finished product. Thank you, to Jennifer DeMeglio for her contributions to the logo design of Diamond Mill Press. A special thanks to John Martinetti of JEM Graphics for his hard work on the website. John's enthusiasm and energy are contagious and he has played a major role in my success as an author and growth as a person. Above all else, thank you to my sister Alaina and my parents Louis and Linda, for their tireless support, encouragement, and dedication in helping me turn this dream into a reality.

Table of Contents

POETRY

SHORT STORIES

POETRY

An Uneaten Breakfast

A Work of Art

I hold a land bound by leather and gold,
One that offers all temporary reprieve,
Endless riches for all to behold,
Riches no eyes, mind, or soul can believe.

Continual gates upheld to all
Who wander lacking time or cause,
A flat terrain, peace enthralled,
Heals sins of minor major flaws.

Forgotten tales where struggles rage,
Some lay victored while some unsolved,
One among a thousand of unturned page,
The wanderers find heavy hearts absolved.

Joseph Anthony

<u>When the Sun Sets</u>

A feast for any eye to see
In staring out at the ocean,
From the height of the nine story balcony,
All movement appears in slow motion

Unyieldingly in sets of three
Wave after wave is folded,
In and out, then back to sea
As the mighty power's emboldened

Gulls fly high but underneath
My feet without a glancing
To the view they have as their pattern wreaths,
The scene's beauty they are only enhancing

Golden rays land softly on
The people that they have speckled,
One by one they all are gone,
Now clear is the sand they once freckled

The line across the sky,
Where the water meets the sun,
Vanishes from eye again
And another day is done.

The Swordsman's Locket

A picture in a locket embroidered with such care,
The love one searches a lifetime for hangs picture next to hair,
Life extracted off the top of one who'll never die,
Repaying all that mock his love, in judgment never wry,

A mortal man no God can touch, by all peasants revered,
Swiftness matched by only one, meriting all kings' fear,
With utmost poise upon horseback, making way village by village,
Pliant in scheduling of his day, though never one to pillage,

The metal which hangs around his neck and that that readies his side,
Convey all that a man should be, two things they fail not provide,
Strength from deep within himself, never so prior abound,
And the soul of the loveliest other, a lover's ever found.

Joseph Anthony

May They Smile

Should I let fall ink from my quill and meet
What poison 'waits in my head?

Or would it be better left unsaid? Or
Liquefied in red, when life's absence leaves
My body dead?

Could all the leaves that fall in fall
Stand high and proud and tall
If they met my open eyes prior covered
By a shawl?

May all that watch my strength retire,
Lips pull as lungs respire, smile
For a while before they rest
Flame gently to the pyre?

The Waiting Game

It was a mild childhood friendship, slowly iced by time.

Graduation happened and the two never met again,
Until one day in a doctor's office, when names sounded familiar
    and then:

"I say, that name I've heard before, way back many years,

We have so much to catch up on now," the doctor happily stated,
Then he proceeded to brag a little, of the life for himself he'd
    created.

The patient became impatient and this the doctor noticed,

So he changed the subject and cut it short, hoping he hadn't been
    vain,
"Tell me now of you, my friend, and all of the things you have
    gained."

Things had not wound up the same for the two; this they both
    would realize.

"Well you see..." his voice trailed off, but the man had finally
    spoken,
"...I've second guessed myself too much, and me the world has
    broken."

His embarrassed eyes shifted to the floor, but he continued on,

"For I am nothing more than an almost penniless waiter.
You save lives, are appreciated, and to dinner needs I cater."

The doctor's self confidence quickly turned into pity.

"Now, now. That isn't true," to the waiter here he pleaded,
"You see, both of us have a job and therefore are much needed."

The man rose up and extended the doctor his hand,

"This appointment's over, nice to see you." He intimidatedly
    stated,
He walked away unsure of himself and on tables forever he
    waited.

Wake, Oh Weary Dreamer

Wake, oh weary dreamer, to this storm the day has assigned
While the sun is out, offshore trouble happily looms
With unwavering confidence while the waves do wind.

An endless repetition unlike any of its kind,
Make way to the window in the corner of your room.
Wake, oh weary dreamer, to this storm the day has assigned.

Trance off to the distances where you will be inclined
To slumber on your feet so sleep's picture can resume,
With unwavering confidence while the waves do wind.

Clouds sway low looking dark, yet in them silver some find.
The optimist's outlook helps when picking through the brume.
Wake, oh weary dreamer, to this storm the day has assigned.

Hesitation is normal still, sometimes it may bind
The petals of a flower in its delicate time of bloom,
With unwavering confidence while the waves do wind.

The rainiest day awaits you, bar you should remind,
Night time offers passing shelter from the water's gloom.
Wake, oh weary dreamer, to this storm the day has assigned,
With unwavering confidence while the waves do wind.

Joseph Anthony

When I and My Long Love Had Parted

When I and my long love had parted
    In hand I left with ardor's pill,
They say breaking grows easy once started,
    Though to me it felt harder still.

Levity left from this consoling
    Was transient as passing breeze,
Better days I went extolling,
    Living present with love's disease.

Preface to a Twenty Volume Life Memoir

After Amiri Baraka

A long time ago, I'd grown used to the way
Kite flyers on the city sidewalks
Hid the sun on my walk home from work.
Their unforgiving strings hissed—
Fewer people seemed to smile...

Things had come to that.

And then, each day I would count the kites
And each day I would get a smaller number.
And then there were none to be counted,
So I would count my homeward steps.

Nobody flew kites anymore.

And then one day I tiptoed down
To the church and prayed next to a little girl
Who was gone when my eyes opened.
I cracked the door to leave and saw her there...
Just she on the sidewalk, gazing up

With kite string in her hands.

Joseph Anthony

The Loner and the Shepard

"The People come—and with them grief,"
      A Loner said in disbelief.
"Eyes narrow and noses raised,
      Invaluable values lowly appraised."

"They flatten my grass," the Shepard spurned,
      "With feet unfit to quench their own thirst—
More and more each spring return—
      What can we but expect the worst?"

The Loner defended, "Fault them not,"
      But the Shepard cut him with "—you're wrong.
I've made my pass, and I cannot,
      My sheep are safe but not for long.

"You don't believe in my believing
      That broken trust is beyond repair,
They who appear dear can be deceiving
      —the good in you does not compare."

"I do believe," the Loner extended,
      "That faith is wonderful when shown."
With that the conversation ended.
      The Loner wandered off alone.

To Memory

When I had finished painting, Memory
Sat for coffee with me
And we spent hours talking
She made me laugh
She made me cry

The time passed fast
As
She and I
Danced together
On the floors of my mind.

There were holes in those floors
And from time to time
She fell through them

Down another flight
To
Another story

Holding my hand as I followed
In and out of the hollow rooms
To the cluttered rooms
Where she laid her baggage out and agreed to stay the night

I kissed her wet
Ruddy lips just before
She pulled back and asked
Me
If I remembered her

Yes
I said

How could I not?
We had spent so many nights dancing
Holding twisting
Each other as we did now

I did remember her
Even though
Her face was always changing

Changing with the wallpaper of every room

An Uneaten Breakfast

Missouri Tears

You say you dream of Cali where the sunshine never ends,
But baby it won't do you justice,
Because let's face it, you look even better in the night.

West coast trips last forever, dreamers dream
Not only when darkness descends.
Rather with persistence, as in the blackest of
Skies the stars shine bright.

There can be little done to bring us together.
At least for now in two directions we are uncertainly bound.
My life seems rooted in the gravel along the outskirts of
The city that sleeps no more.

Our hands may fit freely; however, the hands of time
Are tightly wound.
But don't be surprised one morning to find me at your door,
With much more promise for you than I could ever promise you
before.

Joseph Anthony

Underneath the spiny trees,
Colder just a few degrees,
Brows were wiped clean in the shade,
While sipping mouths of lemonade.

The grass dark green in fresh cut smell,
Two seasons prior to the birds' farewell,
A truck passed through with Italian ice,
Selling at less than asking price.

There was a park where children played,
And by night crickets would serenade.

Now the spines have curved and limbs are bare,
The shade is gone, to all despair,
The grass has browned and is not well kept,
Beaks have fattened and are inept.

Tongues are unsoothed by flavors so cold,
The tires have worn and children grown old,
Though what touches deepest those of the past,
The crickets' song was compromised last.

In Memory of Vinnie and Mike

good morning, fragile Life.
or so it seems.
your eyes look red, from crying?
no,
but today will undoubtedly be wet.

sleep in as morning passes on…
early birds don't fare-well against
that crooked Eagle.

don't make that great escape
and leave us
with bitten tongues,
unable to say goodbye.

fragile Life,
you leave a hollowed out feeling
of inexpressible emotion
that is unbearable for too many people.

cloudy eyes under teary skies,
it's too early to say goodnight
to fragile Life.

Joseph Anthony

Sum of Parts

An old man waited at Heaven's gate,
Hat in hand while sitting.
In quarrel, immortals debated his fate
Accusing and acquitting;
His life had been neither poor nor great,
In equal direction the vote went splitting:
There are no rules high in the skies,
Where sacred contemplation lies.

He followed not the word of the lord,
But broke it only a few times, if ever;
He strayed from good when he was bored,
But slept with evil less than never;
He stole only what he could not afford,
But was caught often for not being clever:
There are no rules high in the skies,
Where sacred contemplation lies.

It's unimportant what they decided
When all was accounted for and weighed;
Deeds and misdeeds had been collided
And of their decision, he wasn't afraid;
He was but one man, undivided,
By the decisions in his life he made:
There are no rules high in the skies,
Where sacred contemplation lies.

An Uneaten Breakfast

Hold Me Not In Times of Pain

Hold me not in times of pain, though thou think I need be held,
Ere I'm to walk hand upon thine, these hearts of two lovers must
meld,

For any passion blossomed surely, at such a rapid rate,
Is harsh doomed prior the beginning, of its short lived dilate,

Spite my pride not in vain, so honor I may keep,
Not to steal a single kiss, when parallel we sleep,

A lifetime full myself devote, I pledge to thee my word,
To sing each night the purest song, ears man nor beast have
heard,

Come the sunrise of our end, my time in thy arms just begun,
Weep sweet tears whilst finger tips meet, as two souls live on as
one.

Joseph Anthony

Violet on the Ocean Floor

Violet on the ocean floor
Lie still while the waves are breaking.
Wash upon the shallow shore,
Violet on the ocean floor,
Head back to where you lived before
Your petals started aching.
Violet on the ocean floor,
Lie still while the waves are breaking.

True Love said to Destiny

True Love said to Destiny,
"You bring out the best in me."
Destiny replied,
"Long I've loved and long I've tried
To hide myself from others who
Don't know the world as I or you."

Long hair the color of a dove,
"They search for me," continued Love,
"In every face that passes by,
Waiting for eternity,
Many weep when I they nowhere find
And now and then they call me blind."

"Of nothing more I've e'er been sure,
Your eyes are fine, your heart is pure,"
Said Destiny proceeding on,
"What's found then lost is never gone."

Love wholly agreed in half silent prayer
If once she was present, she'd always be there.
"In truth, by God we both are strong,
Though one may fade away erelong."
"It's not wrong for one to want for us two,
To live long with me while fulfilling you."

Spoke Destiny in softest way,
"Never far from you I'd stray
Were I not called o'er every sea,
To live this just indignity."
"Hopeless are those," True Love outcried,
"Who've not yet met me by the time you've arrived."

Joseph Anthony

He Who Pays

He who pays respect to a friend,
Once known back many years,
Is met with sadness, nothing more then,
Failing in forcing a lonely tear.

He who pays respect to a brother,
For whom tough love was defined,
Is met with pride unlike any other,
In both childhoods that are intertwined.

She who pays respect to a son
As a mother who raised him well,
Is met with embrace by all but the one
She has to bid unbearable farewell.

He who pays respect to a son,
As a father who praised him not,
Is met with regret that is only outdone,
By the undelivered love his boy never got.

He who pays respect to a foe,
Long after bitter struggles have ended,
Is met with accepting glances, although
Forgiveness is not the reason he attended.

He who pays respect to a stranger
He has never seen or known,
Is met with applause by He in the manger,
And will never be alone.

There's a Lizard in the Children's Room

There's a lizard in the children's room,
High up on the wall.
Mother tried him with a broom
But the little guy refused to fall.

Sometimes I go in and stare at him,
Though I cannot recall,
One so still in face and limb
Of stature quite so small.

His patience dignifies him
In ways too tall to tell,
No loudness or light succeeds to surprise him,
In discipline he's doing well.

The children call his name you know,
High pitched voices too low to be heard.
He's family now, as far as families grow,
To bother him would be absurd.

His back is black as night's not white,
Grey is his tummy now like the wall,
And mother since has grown to the sight,
Perhaps she likes him most of all.

For he has never spoken ill-ly
Of a single creature on this earth,
He judges not and never will he
Disvalue play where play is of worth.

Joseph Anthony

Lilac Hair

She offers so much more,
Possesses so many traits
That mankind hasn't seen before.

That faintest hint of a smile
Reveals virtue and mischief,
While she peeks through bangs of lilac hair.

She's no fairytale princess,
That comparison is unjust.
She's sprinkled with imperfections
That hide in her lilac hair.

A radiant summer birthday,
Outdoes those of December.
Lush skin and tender-faced,

Beautiful over any other,
Yet still just more than a child.
One with lilac hair.

Moving gracefully—
Playfully—
She outdoes every flower,
With her lilac hair.

2's & 3's

They say that bad things come in 3's and not 2's,
But I'm in too good a mood to sit wording blues.
That's one already baby, I'm on my way down,
I only think of you when no one else's around.

That's 2 in itself since you're never home,
The 3rd half is found in my being alone.
Grounded so easily, I guess that it's true
Bad things come in 3's instead of in 2's.

They say good on the other comes in 2's and not 3's.
This also has truth, that's not hard to see.
I've been high before and will be soon again,
There's 2 without trying, when wording blues ends.

The math isn't tricky, you always end low
And that's as far up as the numbers will go.
You'll always have lost before you've begun,
3's higher than 2 and 2's never won.

The Broken Cinquain

Distance
Moves between us,
Spreading his arms out wide,
Transparent, it's apparent we're

Alone.

For Chris

I   'm not so sure of details, for this boy I did not know.

W hen Heaven holds a vacancy a halo must be pressed,
I   roned to perfection, worn by the eternally blessed,
L ittle did I realize upon hearing of his death, a new angel was to
     be crowned,
L o and behold I took notice, with feelings so profound.

W ayne Valley bore the image to me, as a place like all the same,
A nd since then we can both agree, that different it became.
T o say that I am jealous now, of the town, would be quite fair,
C ause never have I felt the closeness of friends as I would have
     had I lived there.
H umbling times try our faith

O nly to be warded off by the teachings the departed leaves, for
V ery little cannot be done, by someone who believes.
E ach future we're reminded is fragile, and not so guaranteed,
R aw emotion speaks the truth, and tears that truth did breed.

Y ears to come may threaten memories; however they'll fail to
     erase
O ne rule: follow not your dreams, instead lace skates and chase.
U nder different circumstances I would have been a friend of
     Chris

- but honestly, if he were here, I think he'd tell us this.
C ommon interests bring forth friends, as opponents on the ice
     we touched gloves.
K indness from a stranger can be the simplest form of love.

In Memory of Chris Krassowski

Joseph Anthony

Orange Groves

If you're ever in the orange groves alone,
While admiring how the fruit has slowly grown,
Take notice of the shadows on the ground;
How the darkness hits the floor and rebounds,
How they shade the dirt that isn't sown.

A trader would never mistake a gold coin for a stone,
And the baker, never a cupcake for a scone.
If you know your body, the differences resound
In the subtleties that separate us all.

Before you leave the orange groves for home,
Take notice where the planter's tools are thrown,
Like secrets, hid under a tree so they do not confound
The beauty of the rows when no one else is around.
With humility the imperfections are shown
In the subtleties that separate us all.

Rainbows in Raindrops

When you look in raindrops for rainbows
You find millions of tiny pots of gold.
Keep confidence high and worry low,

Whether you search fast or gaze through them slow,
There are so many fairytales to be told
When you look in raindrops for rainbows.

Clouds do not care what lies below.
When dropped in water uncontrolled,
Keep confidence high and worry low.

Think highly, as far as high thoughts will go,
You never know what can be foretold
When you look in raindrops for rainbows.

Good fortune is liberally bestowed
To those who seek what is not sold,
Keep confidence high and worry low.

Melting icicles have a tendency to show
Warmth can still be felt even if you are cold.
When you look in raindrops for rainbows,
Keep confidence high and worry low.

What Need My Love?

Name your needs, my Love of loves,
    So I may alleviate your longings,
Or does desire company you
    And provide your mind with sense belonging?

Fault me not in admiration,
    For crafting an eternal shrine
To your beauty, in aging grace
    Certain to withstand the hands of time.

Your troubles set for foreign setting,
    Your jealousors quiver at my hand,
So for your wealth, and fame, and state,
    Kings will make unjust demand.

Mourning with Apollo

When a crisp night had disappeared
We spent the morning drying tears,
Those same ones I'd helped Apollo cry.
And when the last were finally dry,
He smiled, or so it would appear.

A blushing Eos would make unclear
If happiness had taken the place of fear
Or if my efforts had gone awry,
As the wind blew through the laurel's hair.

Apollo spoke to me sincere
In thoughts that struggled to cohere.
Upon their end he said that I
Had earned his immortality.
He touched my hand and left me dear,
As the wind blew through the laurel's hair.

Song Lyrics #3

I'm sorry I can't take this disappointment anymore
I just can't break this habit
I've forgotten where I'm going
Because I can't remember where I've been before

I need closure for a chapter
That I never meant to close
And no one knows the pain
I'm losing my composure
Lost it only as far as not having it anymore goes

Broken bottles broke me further
Spun me farther from the truth
When you can't find all the pieces
It's hopeless
I need no further proof

I'm sorry I can't take this disappointment anymore
I just can't break this habit
I've forgotten where I'm going
Because I can't remember where I've been before

They say that taking chances
Is a bitter part of life
Insecurities got the best of me
The funny thing about romance is
They couldn't be more right

You don't even need to answer baby
What's left is set on walking out the door
Maybe you didn't mean to forsake this
But I can't take this disappointment anymore

Same Year Different Story

Same year different story.
My how time crawls by.
Even paper looks more like snow the longer you stare at it.

Snow melts the closer the calendar turns toward summer,
And it turns like a ballerina doll low on batteries.

Lullabies that used to sound so sweet to us
Don't help us sleep anymore.
Once youth's security is lost,
Nothing is ever as safe as it was before.

But it wasn't safe in the first place.
So a safe isn't safe at all.
An apple only gets bruised if there are no
Leaves on the floor when it fell.

Tense will not matter.
Breaking it only increases tension.
Words are occasionally confusing
And are confused occasionally themselves.

Joseph Anthony

Ship Sails

You cannot strike a dog and expect him to return.
You cannot light a fire and refuse the want to watch it burn.

You cannot blithely walk away, without at least a glancing back.
You cannot tie emotions down, like ship sails after giving them
slack.

Like the wind that turns the ship,
Emotion turns you left or right.
If you could do what you haven't done,
Who knows where you'd dock tonight.

You may have wandered lands from here, or perhaps your bed
would be the same.
You may have found life poor on the streets, or perhaps you'd lie
well off in fame.

This said, you cannot run, my love, as I cannot take leave of you,
Because all ships sail the same ocean, and I know what emotion
can do.

The Cat and the Child

"Oh the places you will go,"
The cat said to the child.
"I hope that you will never know
How it feels to be defiled."

"It's wild that when you've grown old
You'll look back on younger days in regret,
Imagination is a thing to behold
And life is but roulette."

"I'll bet you've seen," the child guessed,
"More than I'll ever get to see."
"Remember the good and forget the rest."
The cat answered quietly.

"To me, a vivid memory
Is but life's greatest curse.
No strife or struggle, you'll one day agree,
Could do you any worse."

The child watched him in confusion.
"The places," the cat continued more,
"Will leave you sad and disillusioned."
"I've been," the kid said, "there before."

"Ah, so you know," the cat said in sorrow,
"And so it is I'm too late then."
He talked to another child tomorrow
And the day after that, another again.

Joseph Anthony

The Perfect Quatrain

Take me to a patient place.
That's right, a peaceful place.
Tranquil in its entirety.
Tonight, tomorrow—eternity.

My Depression

The wine is chilled, the flowers are frosted with snow,
And as you walk in, my emotions, they grow.

As I stare at my depression,
I'm pondered by this mad obsession.

The way that you look in the dim colored light,
The way that your eyes and your lips invite.

The smile that blushes across your face,
Your tenderness and air of grace.

The way the wind shuffles its way through your hair,
My heart fills as a ship does in ocean despair.

The table is set, so my darling let's eat,
Weak in your presence, I'm swept off my feet.

I pray the time comes when I meet your sweet lips
As I wrap my arms around your hips.

Moments as this, though discreet, will be treasured
Alone on this rooftop where we are together.

The music is low as the hours are taken
Away with my hope while reality wakens.

Suff'ring in silence down deep over thee,
For my love lies with you, but yours not with me.

As time circles on, I'm filled with aggression,
All thanks are due, to my depression.

Joseph Anthony

Lady Lilith of Possibility

When it felt like there was nothing more that she could do
She turned herself inside out
And she was beautiful.
Even though the skin she wore was no longer true

Thin whispers of truth hung around her
Adversaries to her every thought
Her every move
Until they wrapped and tightly bound her

The strings pulled through that body leaving
Pieces to the etherized flesh
A few moments left
She spent believing that

Those who spend their lives thinking of possibilities
Get lost in their endlessness
And miss out
On endless opportunities.

World Gone Mad

All poor richen, all rich crawl,
All dumb smarten, all smart fall,

All weak strengthen, all strong bruise,
All losers win, all winners lose,

All tall shrink, all small grow,
All bright darken, all dark glow,

All dirty become cleansed, all clean become foul,
All hunters are hunted, all the hunted on the prowl,

All sick healthen, all healthy get sick,
All fast become slower, all slow become quick,

All dead rises, all life dies,
In a world gone mad, only madness survives.

Joseph Anthony

Tragedy of the Commons

Punishment suffered, though long overdue,
To be rid of the haunting face,
Through my every thought, the image imbued
Of a love I've tried hard to erase.

My fault so sure in being untrue
To a woman I once courted and chased,
In gardens as vast as cornfields in Heaven,
That vanished from my future without a trace.

Her only wish, to be loved by this man
While wrapped in my once tender embrace,
That hardened to sin and has never been pardoned,
Still haunted by that lovers face.

On the evening I spoiled her heart,
No hesitation held back the dagger that laced,
While she fed yet a single line to my ear
In, "you I cannot replace."

To live without me, she decided not,
With a thrust, all we shared was displaced,
Punishment endured, with end long overdue,
Never rid of her haunting face.

Where Have All the Flowers Gone?

Hand in hand I walk with he, our fingers intertwined,
Magically he smiles at me, unconditional love here defined.
My greatest work of art by far, the pride of all my years,
With the simplest reassurance, I can ward off all of his fears.

This little one that walks with me at a fraction of my height,
Knows no limits to his dreams, which eagerly I do incite.
These eyes radiating innocence will be extorted over time,
Bar for the moment no truer word exists to this young boy as
mine.

Any want or need of me, I walk through fire to provide,
And questions that he does hold, I try best to conquer then
divide.
So "where have all the flowers gone?" should be simple enough
to say,
But after searching silent thought, an answer I cannot convey,

"I'm not quite sure, lad, that I know," while bending to a knee,
Upon arrival face to face the one hath turned to three,
"Why'd they need to go away? When again will they come back?"
"Well, you see, the world is full of sad things and meanings for
them it lacks."

Joseph Anthony

The Priest and the Night Dove

I saw before the night dove sang
The fair moon judge the present lost.
Fighting for peace o'er any cost,
The night dove showed his tiny fang.

I lullabied his anger sleep
Before blood stained his snow white coat,
The faintest whistle escaped his throat.
Peace he'd found and peace he'd keep

Had not a man perceived as blessed
Prayed to the judge for more unrest.

Phantom

I'll turn this darkness into a light of gold before the night is
    through,
I write my best depressed like this, when I start remembering
    you.

I've learned a lot in my throughout years, though I've never
    learned from the past,
A purity may appear certain, but what's certain never lasts.

Words are born from the air we breathe and that's all they are
    when broken down,
There isn't need to dress them up in diadem or crown.

A chronic case of apathy, my Freudian defense,
Content with desolate emptiness, unhindered and immense.

Relinquishment of all control to the numbness live within
That aggregates a phantom where a romantic once had been.

I'll work this darkness into a good thing before the night is
    through,
And I won't for a while after I'm finished, but this page will
    remember you.

Joseph Anthony

A Deaf Blind on the Train Tracks

A man that has lost his ears and his eyes
Knows not what he hears on the tracks and dies.

My Colors Fade

My colors fade as each new sun declines
And life's trek pulls me farther from my home.
Try as they may, the stars can't seem to shine
As they do in a land not far from Rome.
The towers glow against the crescent moon,
The gates stand tall protecting what's behind
From the Governor, whose robbers swoon
To loot the students of all they can find.
A worthy man is he who sails the ships,
To bring Manuel's work 'cross the hemisphere—
And any brother who should fall or slip
Will be pulled up and lovingly endeared.
      After I pen this ritual by hand,
      May none rest 'til it's done throughout the land.

My colors fade as each new sun declines
And life's trek pulls me farther from my home.
Try as they may, the stars can't seem to shine
As they do in a land not far from Rome.

Joseph Anthony

The Tale of Princess Elizabeth Jade

A princess long her father's strife
No suitor taker her for a wife.
Was placed at last in the highest of towers,
To be mourned by only malting flowers.

Upon one ball, musicians playing
Ceased, when they heard horses naying.
Then in came one who'd been delayed
And asked for Princess Elizabeth Jade.

The man was young, no more a score who spoke of her lovingly.
The people cheered his determination to rein with her for
eternity.

The king returned at morning next day
To where she'd since been locked away.
In sight, white, her breathless body kept
He touched her hand and there he wept.

With the news the prince left soon after he laid,
A kiss on the lips of Elizabeth Jade.

Wingman

They call me Wingman, soldier of the social realm,
Unstoppable. Uneasily overwhelmed.

I make the untouchable reachable
And who should be unreachable, attainable.

I make sustainable
The moments that are fast to fade away.

They call me Wingman
for my speed
At making strangers not seem strange to
One another anymore.

I'm not in it to win it, but I'll spin it for you.
Placing things that may or may not be true
In the best light possible.

They call to me, Wingman,
When they need an awkward moment cast aside,
Or a line cast into a new sea of fish,

Because with a success rate of four to five,
The only way they are sleeping alone tonight
Is if they are the ones to blow it.

Joseph Anthony

Divine Pride

Deep inside the spider caves,
Far beneath the ocean waves,
There lies a chest with fire flies,
The glow as pure as the sun's slow rise,

Guarded by two blades of steel,
Bound by rope from heel to heel,
Leather is stripped and slowly dried,
Folded over and carefully tied,

Flowers drape across the box,
And at the base lie jagged rocks,
Cuts so deep from slices of paper,
Covered lightly with water vapor,

Animals slumber in their beds,
Quilts are woven with tiny threads,
Wood is warped while fires burn,
On the ship from bough to stern,

Each sight picked so carefully,
Long to live by high decree,
Mysterious ways go understood,
As constant battle 'tween Evil and Good,

But of all this, to his friends God raves,
Deep inside the spider caves.

The Mask and the Man

The man in the mask…doesn't need to be understood.
The man in the mask…would strip his face away if he could.

The mask doesn't want to be seen.
The mask doesn't want to be left behind.

The man and the mask are caught in between.
The man and the mask are deeply intertwined.

The man forgets the way his own face looks.
The man remembers that he doesn't care.

The mask forgets he's fastened with hooks.
The mask remembers, of this the man is unaware.

The mask that hides the man…is faded from the sun.
The man that wears the mask…can never be outrun.

Joseph Anthony

A Body of Blight

I've tried talking through words though I can't feel my lips.
I've tried walking round words though I can't move my hips.

I've tried crying 'till calluses cripple my fingers
Against my eyes, where my longing for you lingers.

Left ribs badly bruised, so deep they've been broken,
Lo wait, of this hurt, I've whole heart'ly misspoken.

An Uneaten Breakfast

My Faithful Friend

Hold my paw old friend,
Lend a smile to my eyes.
Hold back nothing you feel my friend,
As we say our goodbyes.

No sorrows please on either side
As I go to sleep,
Just pictures in the memories
I trust you'll always keep.

Gone for good, just in form,
My spirit lives at side with you.
Before I go, my one request
Leaves able task at hand to do.

You've given me the warmest of lives
So please do not stay sad for long,
Pass on my home, food, and fresh water,
Should another in need come along.

Your voice is all I need my friend.
My love for you—undying.
As yours for me, I surely can see,
Your smiling eyes have been crying.

Joseph Anthony

<u>The Child and the Butterfly</u>

A child held a caterpillar and watched him slowly grow
Into a handsome butterfly
That blended with the snow
A child held a butterfly and watched him slowly grow
Tired of his plain white color and then begin to glow
Like all the fireflies of young July
A child held a firefly and watched him slowly grow

The Unaccepted

Hush little one.
don't make a sound.
all who wish to hold us back sleep with their ears pressed to our
locked door tonight.

And in the smallest of sounds that escape us,
they find the greatest sadness
because we stand for all they wish they were,
and when we're together, we have all they wish they had.

Let's stay quiet for as long as we can,
allow them to fall asleep.
only then can we speak freely without knowing that
our words inflict our antagonists pain.

What shame they preach upon themselves,
living with pride, with hate, in envy.

Oppressive fear fails to bind us, though at times
we wrongly do submit to its limits.

Speak little one.
Speak of all your dreams, desires, and longings.
We've done our part in being kind (with our patience)
But if our voices should wake them,

justice will be served.

Joseph Anthony

Days Like Today

In the fading moments of a sunset
  As we share tiny kisses in the breeze,
Breaths grow heavy against the onset
  Of troubles thus far we've appeased.

Minutes dwindle down to seconds
  Blushing with shy remorse for their speed.
While they pile high our mood swings low
  Grasping them until to dusk we heed.

We are able not to part one another,
  There is very little said or to say
Because days like this are unfairly uncommon
  In the unjust world we live in today.

Better Freddie than Teddy

There once lived a man
named Smellsalot Teddy
who ran and who ran

at a pace always steady.
He never would shower after all his running
and neither would Freddie,

though his hygiene was stunning.
Teddy would praise him
with words so becoming,

For it truly amazed him
his friend never offended.
How so, oh it crazed him

every time he commended,
asking his friend how he always did and still does it
and Freddie said it depended

on who does and who doesn't
take time to complain
how it looks, well because it

is frowned upon and even considered insane,
But it's far better to run when you run in the rain.

Uneasy Tranquility

Red flags mark no swim zones, and seagulls play tag in between
    them.
The sharkless Water begins to talk
Across empty sand to the lonely Boardwalk,
"Our beach lies with dry eyes and none are here to saline them."

"The sun is high, yes hot it is, but we have greater problems it's
    true."
The Walk replied in downcast voice,
Continuing, "I have no other choice,
Than to warp out my days, used, here alone with you."

"Greater problems…" the Water mused, before the Sand spoke
    in defeated cry,
"Perhaps they've finally found better things to do, than visit you
    or I."

Song Lyrics #5

I looked in your eyes last night
While we walked in the moonlight
On the streets of New York, in the crowds
Looking up at the stars our hearts broke for the clouds

I was feeling the sky grow sad
And wished he had what I had
He was so alone,
Without love or a home
So I invited him back to sleep with you and me
Before we happened to stop and see that he
Was growing angry
Growling down from up high, in a roar
All the people before went in and shut their doors
So I said that we should stay out
You agreed but held your doubts
We ran through the rain
No stresses could restrain
It was a freedom unlike anything we've ever known

Tell me baby have you ever felt like this?
Only when I was young
And fairytales were still sung
Tell me baby do you think that we're remiss?
We'll be fine
(We'll be fine)

I can't believe that the stars have gone
The sun's been drawn with crayon
Look how our bodies have both become cartoons
In this new world we are safe, happy, loved, and immune
From all who want to bring back our strife
And troubles of that old life
There's no way we can know

Joseph Anthony

What lies ahead below
As we slide down a rainbow and make this place our new home

Tell me baby have you ever felt like this?
Only when I was young
And fairytales were still sung
Tell me baby do you think that we're remiss?
We'll be fine
(We'll be fine)

An Uneaten Breakfast

<u>Dust</u>

Touch my cheek sweet Angel

                        Leave your fingerprints in magic white
Dust

Drag your fingertips down
My forehead

Past my eyes   over my nose

To my lips

        Pause there

I kiss them.

With wings upon your back
Guide me through this labyrinth

With a glint of evil in your smile

                    Leave me if you must

Joseph Anthony

To the Girl with My Heart on Her Sleeve

There have been many nights where my love for you has grown
While by fireside to your picture I have crooned
In the memories you've cast away and thrown
As the unfair dawn does daily to the moon.

When I was a little boy my father used to warn
That what we hold close at the moment may someday be far,
Leaving in its place where beauty once adorned
A mirror to the past in an even more beautiful scar.

Life's a betting game, won only by those who take a chance.
I placed all that I had on you, in tearing down my parapets
This gambler that garnered up the courage to make an advance
Turned out avoiding regret to meet regrets.

Don't guard your own as excellently as I have done
Only to march it off with someone else to war,
Because if they, as I have, jump the gun,
It may never be as whole to give as it once was before.

Senseless
_____

I've shaken the calloused hands of men
With horses in their throats
And when I asked them all to sing of life,
A few could hit the notes.

I've seen young girls in tulip beds
With bows tied through their hair
Turn from dreaming of princes
To live lives in despair.

I've smelt the ashes of a hushed volcano
That long ago had roared,
Until age got the best of him
And left him 'lone to snore.

I've tasted lips that tasted of tears,
Laced in pain and dipped in sorrow
And turned them into penny candy
And saved them for tomorrow.

I've heard that life is so unfair and never
Was promised or meant to be so,
But had I trusted sense before,
A fair life I would not know.

Certain Addiction

The only thing certain about my addiction is that I am addicted.
Addiction is something that a person cannot control.
If this is true, then why have I been convicted
When nothing about my addiction is certain, except that I am
    addicted?
Pass judgment only to have inaccurately depicted
The person you damn, instead of choosing to extol.
Another thing that's certain is that you think I choose to be
    addicted,
But addiction is something that a person cannot control.

Lay Them Gently

She lays them gently on the ground
For everyone to walk by.
As the sun casts uneven shadows,
She turns her head without a sound
And knows that it is alright to cry.

Blades of grass start peeking through,
Out from the chunks of peaceful Earth,
As the sun casts uneven shadows
On the resting place of this love she barely knew,
In a bond that started before birth.

She kisses the cross of stone
Lovingly, with tender lips,
The shadows get greater with the sun's disappearance.
As the breeze passes, she knows she's not alone,
And her pain she strongly grips.
Lay them gently.

Joseph Anthony

<u>If You Don't Believe Me Ask a Poet</u>

If you don't believe me, you should ask a friend
Why truth is all but impossible to find.
Because lies always hold a purpose to defend
The goods and evils that they stand behind.

If you don't believe me, you should ask a doctor
Why the deadliest form of cancer is cancer of the mind.
All the therapy in the world cannot alter
It's course, once the virus has started to unwind.

One rock is taller than the rock that lies below it,
As an unsolved riddle weighs more than all the answers
        combined.
If you don't believe me, you should ask a poet
Why they're the only ones who aren't blind.

Song Lyrics #911

Last night I laid my head upon your pillow
And smiled as I smelt it
A tear rolled down my check to where yours should have been
And in my heart I know you felt it

Stars that fade and those that shimmer out
Are gone but not forgotten, as are you
In a world without peace I'm able to find peace
In my day dreams and the memories of the days we knew

There's nothing harder than moving on
When all you've ever known is what you leave behind
This road is not easy
But at the end of it, I know it's you I'll find

Last night I laid my head down upon your pillow
And laid there as I prayed to Heaven's ears
A tear rolled down my cheek to where yours should have been
And in my heart I knew that you could hear

Joseph Anthony

Lazy Lions

Lions lain out on the flatland
A summer dark in June
With gentle eyes limed freshly
By the ever sorrows of the moon

Lions jaws stretched widely
As yawns spread wings and swoon
In and out of their bellies,
Slept the sorrows of the moon

Lions paws crissed crossingly
Each hair shaked as they shook
Dirty manes from to to fro
Beneath the sorrowful crescent hook

Lions voiced opinions so
Uniquely tuned in tone
Then light came upon the night
And the lions lain as stone.

Mother

Simply an unbreakable bond,
Unequaled by any other,
But yet complex in many ways,
The connection between child and Mother.

Growing and raising young ones,
Nurturing their wings,
Though what matters most to little ones
Are all the little things.

Moments that seem to go untold,
Like cuddling when the child is sick,
Protection from the world on stormy days,
With thought always honest and quick.

Affection birthed in hugs and kisses,
Always there in mass supply,
Yet standing your ground at just the right time,
When the child chooses to defy.

The poet lacks the words to say
All you mean to my sister and I,
For a mother's advice is a precious thing,
And on it we always rely.

Resting a tired head on your shoulder,
Sharing of laughs that long rejoice,
The sweetest sound that there is to hear,
Is that of a Mother's voice.

Waves

```
      luent            is no              em.
     aff  wa          ply  med          th   Em
     the     ves      sim   icine        into    br
    fear     of     ere          for    Give      ace
   not       re   Th            the   ent.          th
  Do         gret.             curr               em


        they    not      you.        that     ebb
    and    will    drown    Accept    they


      boats           life.            the si
     life  to         of  You       when  ght
    No    esc   ecpt   shou     wn      of
   flow.   ape  asp        ldn't  do        dolp
  and         this          feel            hins


          fins          you   failed              or
    holding    reminds    of       relationships,


      ships           swim       Not
     on   ne         ey   too    ves. ev
    ati   ver   Th         in  wa     en
   rel         had.            the        they


          escape
     can          them.
```

The Sky Said to His Restless Bride

The Sky said to his restless bride,
"I'll always have you by my side,
For all to see, I'll keep you near,
If health or illness should appear."
"My dear," his love spoke now in shimmer,
"Your outlook's bright, but mine's much dimmer.

"I'm as unseen as a man without strife
In such this unforgiving life.
Your wife should be as prominent as you,
Perhaps the Ocean would better do."
Hesitation passed between their words,
While both took notice of the birds.

"You have forgotten," the Sky proceeded,
"For feathers to fly, we both are needed."
He pleaded further, extending his hand,
"Without you my tears will blanket the land,
Until all that can be seen is an ark,
Doomed in stormy waters dark."

The Wind then blushed as sideways she spun,
Changed direction again and thus begun,
"You've won my heart long ago but it's true,
For all to be right, you must remain blue.
In our contentment all else would be lost,
What good comes the lover who dies at the cost?"

Outspoken, the sky played the last ace he held,
A wedding gift given and all doubt expelled.
"My face at times is cloudy by day,
Until the atmosphere fades 'way,
Revealing many a thousand stars,
They once were mine, now they are ours."

SHORT STORIES

The Wedding Gift

The morning of Isabella's wedding day she woke up and had a small breakfast alone. She took the milk out of the refrigerator and poured it over half a bowl of cereal. Then sat down in front of the TV where she forced herself to eat. She was understandably nervous. The last few days had gone by quickly and reality was getting hard to differentiate from her nightly dreams. Even in this haze, Isabella was able to identify something else in her stomach than premarital fear. There was pity where joy should have been and hopelessness where tomorrow should have been.

Leaning back against the couch, she closed her eyes and let herself imagine that she was alone along the edge of a wheat field. To her left was a forest, to her right was the open field, but instead of turning into either, she walked straight up the edge between the two. A deer had just jumped up from under the shallow trees and was turning back to look at her when the phone rang.

"I'll be there to pick you up in an hour." It was Annie, her cousin—her best friend.

As she hung up the corded phone on the kitchen wall, she noticed that there were dishes still in the sink from before she got engaged. A bird was tweeting in the bird house on the windowsill outside of her bedroom window, where she sat and smiled faintly to herself as she pulled the clear wrapping away from her white dress. After it was unwrapped, she hung the dress over the curtain rod where it danced, like a ghost, at the hips. Next she got on her hands and knees and pulled shoes out from beneath the bed until she found her white heels. They were the ones she'd worn on her first date with her fiancé—once upon a time—when they went out to dinner at a restaurant neither of them could afford and afterward dancing at an unpopular club where he'd first made an impression on her heart. He was clumsy, but not afraid to make a fool of himself. The way he moved was too mechanical to have been spontaneous and she could tell that they were steps he'd practiced at home in front of a mirror. The lights reflected off his hair like they might off a pond—fuzzily, dispersed. Pleased with himself, Robert sighed and Isabella found it quite charming that he thought he had danced well.

After the date Robert wondered to himself if she was the one. He was smitten by her beautiful smile and that small nose that moved slightly when she chewed. Although he'd spent most of the night starring into them, on his ride home he could not recall what color her eyes were because he'd been too distracted by the thought of kissing her lips. They may have been twenty-four year olds in graduate school, but on the front porch of her apartment building they were young teenagers—anxious for a kiss to happen—who had forgotten the advice of friends and parents on how to handle such occasions.

"I had a wonderful time," she said to him, twirling her key around in her pocket with her index finger.

"This was the best first date I've ever been on," he said.

He may have been telling the truth, but fear of being too forward got the best of him and a goodnight kiss never happened. Instead they settled for a hug and Isabella was confused as she climbed the stairs and peeked out the window to watch him drive away.

The morning of Robert's wedding day, he was woken up to have breakfast. The woman at his side fed him with tender care while he sat up in his bed. She lifted the cup to his mouth so that he could drink, wiped his lips, and then removed his clothes so that she could do him a great favor.

"Annie called," the woman said. Robert said nothing. Instead of speaking he took a deep breath through his nose and held it. "She said that they would be here in an hour," the woman continued.

"Can you leave the room, please? I'd like to be alone for a while."

The woman hesitated.

"I'll be fine," Robert said.

"Yes, I'll leave, but push the button if you need anything."

"Of course," he nodded, forcing himself to smile.

With this, the woman left the room and walked down the hall back to the nurse's desk where she sat waiting uncomfortably for the bell to ring. Robert waited for her to get far enough away before falling into a fit of violent coughing. It was here in all the privacy a single hospital room could offer that he played his favorite game. Each time he fell into a fit he would guess to himself what color he thought the napkin would be when he pulled it from his face. In his own head, he would keep score against himself. If his guess matched the color of the napkin, he would get a point. If it did not, he would get nothing.

Give me red.

It was green.

Ah, three for nine.

His totaled accuracy for the week stood at thirty-three percent.

Good enough for the Hall of Fame.

There was also a second level to the game he played. At the end of each week he would total up the number of correct guesses and put them up against the total number of correct guesses from the week before. Each time he did this he found that he broke last "season's" record.

I'm like Ruth, smashing my own records. No one's even close.

One of the hardest parts of dying is finding ways to trick yourself into not seeing it as things get worse. Despite his unmatched success at the game, Robert failed at this. He knew that the totals were only going up because of sheer fit volume. It had nothing to do with his accuracy or ability to guess the colors. Each season simply had more at bats than the previous one.

When Annie got to the apartment she found Isabella dressed in her gown. The door was open, something Annie had advised her many times against doing, but her best friend was stubborn.

"You are breathtaking, honey," said Annie.

Isabella was seated across the back of the sofa, facing the door when her friend entered.

"Your dress is as bright as you are, Annie. It's wonderful."

"I'm your something blue," Annie said as she shut the door behind her, locked it, and walked over to hug her friend who did not move from the couch.

"You're biting them again," said Annie as she lifted Isabella's hand up to her face, examining it as if it were a fragile relic.

"Please don't start," Isabella said.

"Well we'll see what we can do."

Annie pulled her cousin by the wrist and led her into the bedroom. She sat the bride to be down on the bed before briefly rummaging through the makeup box on her dresser. After finding what she was looking for, she took Isabella's hand and began to file and paint each bitten fingernail.

"Hold still hun, I don't want to hit the skin."

"You know it doesn't matter."

Annie ignored the comment. When she had finished there was a faint smile on Isabella's face and seizing the opportunity to keep the bride's spirit up, she rose to her feet and pulled her excitedly towards the door, "to your chariot my lady, you wed at noon!"

With this, the women descended the stairs arm in arm, got into the car, and left for the hospital.

Robert was in another one of his coughing fits when his nurse walked in with a lunch tray.

"How are you feeling, Robby?"

"I'm going to the Hall of Fame, Leigh."

"I really wish you wouldn't play that game." She set the tray down on the rolling bed table. "Would you like some lunch before Bella arrives?"

"What's the point?"

"I just thought you might like something to calm yourself while you wait for her. You've been coughing all morning. The doctor says if you keep yourself busy it will keep your fits to a minimum."

"You know there's no point."

"It's peanut butter and jelly, your favorite. I know you like the sugar."

"It's the only thing you people can't screw up around here," he said.

Leigh ignored him, changed two of his IV bags, and left the room before the play fight really began to upset him, like it often did.

When he was alone again he picked up the small plastic apple juice and shook it back and forth in his hand. This was his second favorite game. When he shook the apple juice, tiny bubbles formed on the surface. These bubbles indicated the number of days that he had left. It didn't matter how hard he shook the apple juice. There had been days when he'd shaken it gently and wound up with a lot of bubbles. There had been days when he had shaken it violently and wound up with only a few bubbles. It was pure chance—fate, he allowed himself to call it. Without a way to count the number of bubbles exactly, Robert separated them into very distinct categories. There were the days when there were a lot of bubbles and there were days when there were very few bubbles. Even though the days with few bubbles were difficult, the worst outcome was when the number of bubbles fell in between a lot and a few. Uncertainty is magnified as death approaches. People want desperately to see things clearly with as little doubt as possible as they die.

He unwrapped the cellophane from his sandwich and ate it in small bites while he watched the bubbles in the juice pop one at a time. Leigh often made fun of the way he ate slowly. *Bird man*, she'd call him if he hadn't finished the food on his tray. *I like to pick at it*, he'd say. Or, *you'd need to be a bird to eat this*, if he felt like going back and forth with her. While staring at the juice Robert realized that he had been listening to the sound of high heels on a hard floor. The footsteps echoed off the walls, up to the ceiling, and down the hallway to his room. He knew they did not belong to Leigh; she wore sneakers because she ran around all day at work. It was his Isabella because Isabella always walked faster than most women in heels. She had a very distinct quick two steps, a slight pause, followed by two more quick steps. He felt sorry for Leigh and wondered if she ever got to wear heels like his Isabella.

Robert's veins flooded with adrenaline. His palms were sweaty and his shoulders tensed as he lunged desperately forward for the apple juice and stabbed a shaking finger through the tin foil lid. Pursing his lips, he began sucking at the air before the juice was up to his mouth. He took a sip and swished it around in his mouth and then spit the juice back into the round container. After doing this twice more, Robert took half of a sip, swallowed, and was sure he'd managed to get rid of the peanut butter on his breath. As he set his head back on the pillow he heard the footsteps get close to the door before they stopped, he heard voices, and the steps faded away back down the hall until he could hear them no more.

By the time they got to the hospital it was a quarter past twelve. Leigh was waiting for them at the desk once they got to Robert's wing of the hospital.

"How's he doing today?" Annie asked.

"Just fine. A little grumpy but I imagine one look at you should change that," Leigh said shifting her eyes from Annie to Isabella and then from Isabella down the dress she was wearing.

"Is the Judge here yet?" asked Isabella.

"No dear, not yet but I'm sure he'll make it," Leigh answered.

"I wish he were here."

The Judge was a man with amazing charisma. No matter what the situation was it was difficult not to feel inspired by him. People felt as if they were being lifted to new realms of personal accomplishment just by being in his presence. He was shorter than one might expect for a man of such reputation, but because of this, one often felt an immediate intimate connection with him. When Robert was battling his first spell of depression following the diagnosis, it had been the Judge who motivated him to keep living. Following a child custody dispute in which the young boy had leukemia, the Judge had been visiting a rehabilitation center forty minutes from the courthouse. The child had been playing with the building blocks in the waiting room when the Judge walked in with a stuffed teddy bear that was dressed like a baseball player. The center treated patients of all ages and Robert was sitting in the corner hunched over in his chair, face buried in his hands. Isabella was seated at his side when the boy and both his parents were called in to see the doctor. The only people left in the waiting room were Robert, Isabella, and the Judge.

"You're not alone," the Judge had said. "There are always people with you. Even when all is quiet around you there are many people thinking of you—praying for you. And before you go to sleep each night there is at least one person thinking about you that you haven't thought of in a long time."

Isabella thanked him at the time in a manner that had been intended to get the man to stop talking. Her boyfriend had been upset enough and although the man seemed to have good intentions, she thought it best to not exchange further conversation about such a matter with a stranger.

"You need to get off the ground. If you spend too much time on it you'll get comfortable there," the Judge said before leaving.

Isabella waited a moment before telling her boyfriend that she had to use the restroom in the hall. As soon as the door closed, however, she caught up with the Judge and berated him harshly for being insensitive. The two talked for several minutes before Isabella apologized and returned to the waiting room.

A few weeks later Robert proposed. He also began talking with the Judge on a regular basis.

While Annie talked to Leigh about the whereabouts of the Judge, without thinking Isabella began walking down the hall. The bright lights of the hospital seemed to get dimmer the closer she got to Robert's room. Halfway there she became aware that the other two women were calling out to her, but one foot kept moving methodically in front of the other until she felt a tug on her veil.

"I'm sorry dear, I think it's best to wait until the Judge arrives before you see him."

Isabella turned to face Leigh, "I need to tell him something."

"It's best if you wait until the wedding to see him. You two don't need any more bad luck at this point."

Leigh took the bride by the bare arm to escort her back down the hall to the desk where the Judge had slipped in and was now waiting.

"Ah Bella, it's good to see you. You look radiant," he said, opening his arms to her and kissing her on the cheek. While the two exchanged small talk, Leigh snuck away to retrieve the groom.

When Isabella saw Robert she could hardly tell his skin from the sheets on his pillow. As Leigh wheeled him down the hall the two black dots that were his eyes grew larger and rounder. She could see that the whites around his irises developed a yellow tint to them. Dressed in a full tuxedo, the groom fixated his eyes on his bride's neck. In his mind, he began to undress her, imagining they were alone together and his legs worked well again. He kissed under her chin, down her chest, and paused at her stomach. She was breathing rapidly and by the time Robert found her eyes through her veil, she was crying. It was the first time in a long time that the Judge had gone unnoticed in a room. Had it not been for the flowers he was handing to Isabella from the side, Robert may have never seen him.

"Thank you for being here, Judge," the groom said as he tried to lift himself up in the bed as best as he could.

"No need to thank me, Robby. Shall we begin?"

Robert nodded and Isabella took his hand as she turned to face the Judge.

"Dearly beloved we are gathered here today to join Robert and Isabella together in holy matrimony. It is here under the eyes of God, before these assembled witnesses, that we shall join these two together. I understand that you each have prepared something to say?"

Robert turned his head to look for Leigh, who handed him a piece of unfolded paper.

"My Isabella," he cleared his throat, "from the moment I met you I knew that I wanted nothing more than to hold you. I wanted to be as close to you as I possibly could be. Over our last three years together I have realized that no matter how close I get to you I will never have enough of you. When we're apart I'm weak and when we're together you give me the strength to carry on. I feel honored to have been chosen by you and I want you to know more than anything that no matter what happens, I will always be with you. I will be with you forever."

As Robert finished his vow, he lifted Isabella's hand to his mouth and kissed it. It smelled like nail polish and he greedily inhaled—thankful to smell something other than the sterilized air—kissing it again. He picked up a used tissue from his bed and blotted his eyes and forehead. Isabella saw beads of sweat glowing where the bright lights had once reflected off of his dark hair. She squeezed his hand and then released it and exchanged her bouquet with Annie for her own folded paper.

"Robert. I've never met a kinder man than you. The capacity of your heart and the realm of your love are immeasurable. I've also never met a stronger and more courageous man. I cannot stop thinking about you and because of this I know that you will always be with me."

The Judge smiled to Leigh and Annie who were both crying.

"If anyone has a good reason why these two should not be wed, let that person speak now or forever hold his peace." The Judge hardly paused. "Do you Robert take Isabella to be your lawfully wedded wife, to have and to love, to honor and to cherish, in sickness and in health for as long as you both should live?"

"I do."

"And do you Isabella take Robert to be your lawfully wedded husband, to have and to love, to honor and to cherish, in sickness and in health for as long as you both should live?"

"I do."

"Than by the power vested in me by God and the state, I now pronounce you husband and wife. You may kiss the bride."

Isabella leaned down to meet Robert's kiss as the small group applauded. Leigh went to the computer at her desk and out of the speakers came, *I Can't Help Falling In Love With You*. The Judge and Annie helped Robert to his feet and with all the strength he had left in his body the newly wed groom stood before his bride.

"May I have this dance?" he asked.

Isabella's mouth was open and she could hardly contain the joy that made her ribs tingle and her knees weak, "Yes."

With the music playing the two stood rocking back and forth. They were both high off the ground as Elvis serenaded them and everything else melted away like snow. It had been a long time since they held one another. It had been an even longer time since they had had one another. Isabella had known for months now. She had been waiting until Robert needed extra strength to carry on, but she could not keep it from him any longer. She pressed his palm against her stomach and Robert felt a kick in his hand.

They held each other as the song replayed again. Time could do nothing to them anymore. It became irrelevant. At any point during eternity that moment can be revisited and they will both still be there holding onto one another—dancing in place.

A Body in the Woods

I was out hunting a group of men in the woods one af-ternoon. It wasn't difficult at first because a few inches of snow had fallen earlier in the week. Putting my head down and occasionally looking up and ahead in the half circle of my vision, I tracked my prey with a burning hunger in my legs. When the tracks began to cross, as was occasional in the heat of the hunt, I stopped to rub my chin. We had passed the last few hours since school had let out playing like this and it was growing significantly harder to tell the footprints of this game from the footprints of the last. I was eleven years old at the time. Manhunt was a regular activity for me and the neighborhood children no matter the time of year.

Pulling my skull cap from my head while considering which friend to go after, I heard a voice yelling in the distance.

"Tony, Tony!" I heard my best friend Michael calling.

As I took off in the direction of him, his one voice was joined by others who were now calling my name with the same urgency.

When I found the group of seven, they were in a crescent curve, hiding something from my view. As I drew nearer, an opening parted, and eyes widened, waiting for my reaction. I saw there, under the soft blanket of snow, a figure between two thicket thorn bushes. There was a blackness in the center of the body where decaying ribs were visible.

"We need to call my dad," was all I could think to say.

Some of my earliest memories are the days my father and I spent out in the woods chasing deer around our farm. We didn't own the property, but we were the caretakers of it. We lived on it. It was ours. He would button me up in my winter coat and place a wool hat on my head, pulling it down close to my eyes.

"Did you get the apples?"

"As many as I could fit in my backpack."

On days when we planned on looking for deer, he would tell me to get apples or corn. When I got home from school that day, I had gone to the apple orchard at the beginning of the long unpaved driveway. I was seven at the time, but was able to carry the apples of a nine year old. It was a late autumn afternoon, and because it was after the clocks had been turned back, we didn't have as much daylight as we would usually have had. We crossed the small creek that seemed forgotten by the world and peeked our heads where the trail comes out into a rather large field. When I went bow hunting with my father for the first time earlier in that same autumn, we had set up a tree stand halfway up the woods that bordered this field. A massive boulder lay alone in the center of it. The rock had been there long before our family, and there was no explanation as to why it was so misplaced. Because of this rock, which had seemingly fallen out of the sky or grown up from the ground, we called this Rock Field.

We took a brave step off the trail, mindful not to step on any sticks. There was a small doe in the far right corner about two hundred and fifty yards away, feasting on blue grass. I pressed my face into the crux of my elbow to cough and when I did, a great head popped up from the side of the boulder. Foolishly giving our attention to the far right, we hadn't noticed the deer standing just to the left of the rock.

This was Odds, a massive buck that should have been a ten pointer. On his left side, the thick dark antlers would have intimidated even the most battle-tested hunter, but the right side brought a smile to a young boy's face; it was like a sharp spiky hand sticking straight up off of his head, similar to the head feathers on a cockatoo.

My dad motioned for me to stand next to him, and when I did, he unzipped the pack on my back just enough to slide his hand inside. He pulled out an apple and in one motion cut it in half with a knife. Odds licked his nose as he tilted his head. He was about seventy yards away, downwind of us, but in a few seconds he had cut the distance in half. We had done this before and he was just as happy to see us as we were him. It was a game we played with very fragile lines. Now it was my father's move. With half an apple in his outstretched hand, he took a step forward and when Odds did nothing, he took two steps more. My father looked back at me with wide eyes and a look of hope that this would finally be the time he would get the loveable and majestic creature to eat from his hand.

Odds lowered his head halfway before raising it suddenly again as if to say, *that's far enough.* Caught in a trance, my father took another step into the field and the buck turned and scooted back twenty yards. My father dropped the pieces of apple where he stood before turning back to me. We dumped out the rest of the apples in my backpack, our hearts still pounding. When we got back to the trail, I turned around and saw Odds watching us with his beautiful head up and half an apple in his mouth.

I think part of the reason why the farm was always so magical to me was because of how unique it was from anywhere else I had known in the world. There was always somewhere or something new to explore, like the old coop behind the barn, which was one of my favorite places to conquer. Half of the roof had caved in. It had been that way long before I was born, and the red paint on the outside resembled an unfinished puzzle. It was long and narrow, and when I stood in the doorway, I could see the ghosts of chickens running and clucking across the badly splintered floorboards. I was often brave enough to search through it alone during the day, but only went inside at night when I had a friend with me. The individual hen stalls made great bunks when a few of us spent the night there.

My father taught me how to do a lot of things around the farm. We rebuilt the barn one summer, so that the cows would be more comfortable. With huge stacks of long boards and a massive bucket of nails, the skeleton of a shelter formed slowly as the calendar crept toward September. I complained the entire time we worked.

"They're just cows. What do they need a new home for?"

"Those cows are worth more than my car," he said. Something stung in the truth of those words.

Joseph Anthony

It was rewarding when we saw their demeanor and body language improve as they enjoyed their new home. It was funny to watch them run for cover when it started to rain because at first they only walked for the old one with the leaky roof. My father showed me how to chop firewood until my hands were raw and how to cut a field in the most efficient way. I grew to appreciate the things that many take for granted, like the contrasts between the greens and the browns that abundantly compose nature or the beautiful blurry symmetry of trees reflected in a lake. I know that if I live to be very old, it will be in part because of these happinesses.

On the other side of the farm, in the most remote location, there was an old abandoned white house. As far as I know, no one has lived in it during my lifetime. I could tell by looking through the dirty windows that someone long of the past had left a lot behind, as if in a hurry. I would make up stories in my head as to what had driven the people out and away. The only thing that could be more adventurous for a young boy than imagining exploring an old abandoned house would be to actually go inside one. Every time I tried the knob or handles of the doors, though, they were locked. Whenever I asked my father about the old house—who had lived there—if he had a key that worked the locks—he would pretend he hadn't heard me and change the subject. I considered throwing a rock through one of the windows a hundred times, but the fear of knowing too much always held my arm back.

The older I grew, the more I realized how far away it was from everything else on the property. There would usually be no one around it for weeks at a time, and in both my mind and reality, it was the perfect place to commit a crime.

One Saturday morning, after two long hours carrying bags of pumpkin seed from the barn to the seed shack between two fields, I heard a woman's scream. Because I was walking, I was subject to the disorientation that motion throws upon the senses, especially the ears. I swore to myself that it came from that remote part of the property because the sound was faint. I may have been able to shrug it off as a figment of my childish imagination had not the crows answered with repetitive shrieks of their own.

I made a left down a firebreak that cut through the woods as I followed the birds, calling back to them from time to time. I stopped to listen. Panting quietly, I rested my head against my forearm, which rested upon a tree. Seconds passed before I caught motion in my peripheral vision and I was frozen with terror. My boots were heavily anchored into the ground as my eyes widened and my chin tilted back far enough for my mouth to fall open. I saw a face resembling that of an old woman's flying towards me between the flapping wings of an owl. Yellow eyes peered out from the center of dark circles. Its wings flapped very deliberately, as if it were enjoying the way the air felt beneath its feathers. Had the majestic creature not seen me, I can only wonder what I would have done as it came toward me, closer and closer with each flap, not more than ten feet off the ground. Startled by a misplaced human face, it roosted upon a leafless branch and waited with patience that far exceeded my own. I remained still. I turned around slowly. The crows fell silent.

We all stood there, afraid to move for a moment, unable to pull our eyes away from the blackness beneath the ribs that seemed to lead somewhere far beneath the earth. On our way back to my house, Michael explained to me how when he found the body it was just a lump covered by the snow.

"I tapped the center of it with my foot and then I started shouting."

We continued in solemn silence for a while. Not because the visible bone, which was almost as white as the snow, eerily hung over the blackness, but because it was the first unfinished game of Manhunt in the history of our group. The temperature of the air never stopped us. If it was above ninety degrees and humid, we played through the sweat pouring off our bodies. Those who were smart enough to bring two shirts were briefly dry, while those who had only one shirt hung it over a tree branch and wound up with sun burnt backs. If it was below freezing, we wore layers. Some opted for warmth at the cost of flexibility, while others stripped erratically and decided to worry about the flu at a later time. The daylight—or lack of daylight—never stopped us. Games ran late into the night and we reveled in the difficulty of deciphering human silhouettes in the shadows of the trees.

This, however, had been enough to stop us.

It silenced us all because we always took pride in outlasting the elements. We had all carried ourselves through those woods with a cockiness that was now threatened. This feeling strangely managed to hold back the fear and excitement we were all experiencing. My father's green pick-up was parked in the grass where our concrete walkway began as we came within view of the house. We charged the lawn, some faster than others, forming a screaming mob of children that drew my father out and down the front steps of the porch.

"Tony, what's going on?" he asked.

"There's a body in the woods. Mike found it. We were playing Manhunt," I panted.

A slight raise of the eyebrows was his only response. He ordered everyone but Michael inside and made it clear that he wanted no one back outside until we returned. Michael and I escorted him into the woods, one of us on each side, and found our way back with strange ease.

"Stay here," he said as he approached it. Mike and I looked at one another, swallowing our tongues. My father paused where we had formed the crescent a little while ago. He stepped closer and I began to scan all I could see around us to make sure that we weren't being watched. With brute disregard, he began to push aside the thicket on the left with bare hands. *The thorns must feel like razors*, I thought.

"Come here, boys."

I shot Mike a nervous look, but did not receive one back. Instead, his eyes were glazed over and his feet were moving mechanically forward in a zombie-like manner. I took a deep breath and held it as we peered through the razor bush to see what we were meant to see. Sticking up out of the snow, hidden by both the sticks and the unimaginable excitement we had felt when we first found the body, we saw antlers.

"It's a deer, boys, that's all. Michael, go back and get my saw from the shed."

Disappointment and relief wrestled with each side of my body, but it was fear that retook me as an important question came to mind.

"How do you think it died?" This wasn't the real question I meant to ask.

"I don't know," my dad answered.

I bit my bottom lip and hesitated before retrying. "Is it Odds?"

"I don't know," he answered again. "Let's take a look."

With this, he went shoulder deep into the razor bush and pulled up on the visible antlers. The head was stuck to the ground and it gave a sticky creak when it was freed. The semi-frozen side of the face was for the most part preserved, but the other half of the face was gone to the point where you could see the deer's bone and teeth. The beam he was holding the head up by had five points and the other side resembled the head feathers of a cockatoo.

Maybe it's a different deer. Maybe it's not the same one, I tried to convince myself. Michael was back with the saw in his hand in less than five minutes. He passed it to me, mirroring my sadness, and I could tell that he was also disappointed that it was not a person.

"How do you think he died?" I asked again, this time wanting an answer.

"I don't know, Tony. He probably just got old and died. That's life. Get over it and hand me the saw."

I relayed it to him. Mike and I watched him cut off the rack. And later that night, I watched my dad apply salt to the raw side of Odds's skull cap.

An Uneaten Breakfast

Prologue: A Preview From The Editor

Writers often speak of being in touch with a subcon-scious zone which enables them to write. This zone comes and goes and at times is extremely difficult to find and control. *An Uneaten Breakfast* is a firsthand glimpse at the life of a tortured man. William Scott's extraordinary talent is showcased by the emotion brought forth from the tortures that this hapless author endures. The results of his hardships provide us with some of the greatest poetry and prose of the pre-depression era. This story, however, is focused not on the famous works of Scott, but on the fuel for the subconscious behind them. Scott has courteously allowed us to publish this revision of *An Uneaten Breakfast*—originally published eighteen years ago in 1923—to include this prologue as well as an epilogue for you, the reader.

Joseph Anthony

An Uneaten Breakfast
-William Scott

When the most precious thing in your world religiously haunts you, it can make life a living hell. If it weren't for the small flicker of hope I squeeze on to, I would end the pain and head there now. It's not that I don't value life; I just place none on my own at the moment. A wise man once said that a life of worth is ill worth living alone. In this I find great truth, but in that truth I find great sadness. If I had known at that moment that I might never see or touch him again, I would have held him close and never let go. The last words I said to him allow me some solace to my pain, but his response to those words brings me to tears upon the very thought.

My name is William Scott. I am thirty-six years old and a professional poet. I have always been a gifted writer, but it was not until the worst happened that I would begin to hone my skill. And then, after the worst occurred, my world ended when the final ray of sun that had shined down upon it, shined no more. The very work I'd honed began to tear me to pieces. Slowly it shredded what there was left to shred of a spoiled heart. I took shelter in the bottle, only to find that with the bottle's help I'd perfected my art, to my publisher's delight.

I was born in 1887 in West Yorkshire, England. I grew up in the small town of Featherstone, where my father was a coal miner. The town held no more than a few thousand people or so, and even though it was small enough for people to get to know one another well, everyone kept mostly to themselves.

94

Our house was old, small, and run down, but at least it kept us dry. The most endearing thing about it was the small stream that wrapped around from the backyard to the side of the house like the leg of a dog. Some of my first memories are of my father taking me to fish by that stream when I was five. I remember his large hands and how they were permanently stained with soot. Featherstone was built on coal mining, so in a way, I can proudly say that my father helped build that town.

He would put me in my boots and when we got to the water we'd stand in the mud along the edge and pick up the sticks that had collected along the sides. We only used the ones that looked straight enough to serve as fishing rods. I'd hold the sticks in my arms and he'd pull out some thread he'd stolen from my mother.

"Shhhh," he'd say as he'd press a blackened finger to his lips. "She doesn't need to know about this. It's just between us boys, okay?"

I would always smile widely when he said that, not necessarily because harmlessly stealing thread from my mother was funny, but more so because his finger would always leave a chalky grey streak from just under his nose down to his chin. He would tie hooks to the thread and the thread to the sticks. After the rods were made, we were ready to start fishing.

It was rare to catch something because the water was shallow. One time, however, after a rather large storm swelled the size of the stream, I felt a huge tug on my fishing stick. I can still feel the rough bark of the pole scraping against my tiny fingers as I leaned and took small steps backward. Even at such a young age, I remember praying for the line to hold.

"That's it, William, you've got him. Keep going, you're almost there," encouraged my father, "just a little further, a little further and—"

"I can't. It'll break. You take it!" My eyes darted from my father to the fish. "You take it, Dad!"

But he wouldn't. He just smiled. While I was pleading for him to take the pole, I had backed up far enough to pull the fish out of the water and into the mud. I vividly remember the look of excitement on his face. Excitement that was even greater than when he caught a fish himself. He reached down and took the fish in his hands and for a moment the world stood still.

I kind of wish that time had not paused for that second, because when it picked up again, it must have thrown me off balance. I took a step toward my father and I slid on the mud, landing sideways in the stream. Most five year olds might have cried a lot longer, but whatever few tears had fallen stopped when my dad handed me the fish.

"It's a pike. Shall we keep him and eat him, or would you prefer to throw him back?" he asked.

"No. I want to throw him back so maybe one day we can catch him again!"

We unhooked and released the fish before picking up the fishing sticks and heading home for supper. I needed to change into dry clothes anyway. As we walked away I had already decided that this was my lucky rod and that I would use it from then on whenever we went fishing behind our house.

When we got in and all sat down together, my dad let me tell my mother the story myself. It was the first story I had ever told, actually. I used every word in my less than extensive vocabulary to tell her all about the epic tale that had just taken place. The only thing that I left out was the part where I had been crying. She didn't need to know that.

It was fourteen years ago—1909—when my wife and I had moved to America from England and I was to publish my first volume. I had requested—rather, been granted—an advance with which we used to cover the move as well as the purchase of a small two-room house. The window held dirty glass and the heavy wooden door was splintering at the bottom. A small garden lay proudly under the window and there was a beech tree in the front yard to the right of the cracked, weed ridden walkway. Mary, my wife, would often sit under it and admire her garden from afar. On tired days, I would sit out there with her and rest my head on her shoulder as her blonde hair tickled my cheek.

"We've come a long way, have we not?" she kissed my hand.

"We have. Remember when we would sit and eat rowan from the trees back home?"

"You miss it, don't you? Home. I can see it in those tired brownie eyes."

I smiled, she read me well. "I miss England, yes. Things were simpler. But I cannot miss home. Home is here." I pointed to our house, "Home is right there."

The success of the book brought stability and a few months later my wife conveyed the magical news that she was pregnant. We awaited our child's arrival anxiously, but it was me who got to enjoy him. His mother experienced complications and although he came in perfect health, she passed away giving him birth. I held my son the night I brought him home from the hospital and we cried together. It was that night between changings, feedings, and tears that I became in touch with my subconscious like never before. The baby would fall asleep in erratic intervals and at these times I wrote instead of slept. Threads of raw emotion were woven deeply into my soul and it was my job in moments of silence to unweave them if I were going to find peace again.

For the next few years, words in poems and stories poured from my heart. As I watched young William—as I called him—grow, he brought me some of the happiest times of my life. The littlest moments made all the difference to me. He helped me get through losing Mary. Those faded green eyes could work miracles. We weren't sure how he got greenies—his mother's eyes were blue and you already know mine are brown. I'm not an artist who paints with color, so I'm not quite sure if mixing blue and brown would yield green. It probably does—at least in that case it did. The fire in my quill began to fade in fatherhood; I had more important things to worry about though. My son was full of questions, questions that I could not always answer.

"Father?"

"Yes, Mary's Will?" which I often called him to remind myself every now and then of my wife. I wanted my son to know his mother's name at the very least.

"Where have all the flowers gone?"

We had been out roving around the nearby flatland. It was nearing the end of fall and the flowers were gone for the winter. He had noticed that the daffodils which sat in the grass along the dirt road a few weeks earlier were now gone. There was concern in his voice. I thought back to the garden that used to lie beneath our window, next to the old door. When Mary passed, her violets and lilies went too.

I hesitated, "Well you see, son, the world sometimes is full of sad things. And meanings for them it lacks."

Young Will had started school and had taken particular interest in writing, as well as the developing field of photography. His writing reminded me of my own as a boy, but I could teach him little about his curiosity for photography. So, for his tenth birthday, I'd bought him a camera. It was a big gaudy thing with a blinding flash, and he loved it. My life, my son, was happy. For his age, he was so smart. He would take pictures of birds, trees, and anything outside. I wasn't sure why he took pictures of these things; if he was going to write about them, he could simply sit outside and write about them, saving film and money. I allowed him privacy, but this I decided to bring up.

"Will, may I be so bold as to ask why you take pictures of these things? I know that you write about them, but why don't you just, well, write about them?"

He giggled, "Why Father, if I take pictures of birds, I can write about birds when it's night."

I was taken aback by the confidence in his voice. Like I said, smart for his age.

A year later, on his mother's birthday, he decided he would teach me the camera.

"Father," he asked, "would it be fine for you to take a picture of me for mother? I mean, wouldn't you think she'd just love to see what I look like today, father?"

Needless to say, the idea was a good one. He showed me how to work the big lug of a camera and he took a seat on the kitchen chair. I flinched as I pressed down on the button, fearing I'd break it. His left arm hung over the backrest. He had a white undershirt on and a long sleeve blue and white checkered cover, dark circles hung under his eyes, and the light of the kitchen candle cast a shadow on the wall behind him. I can describe the picture to perfection from memory because, since that night, it hasn't left me. He was about twelve, eager, and fearless. He insisted that we go show his mother the picture right away. I assured him that we would go first thing in the morning because it was well into the nighttime hours of the day.

"But we have to go now. It's her birthday!" he began to raise his voice. "How can we not give her her birthday present on her birthday?"

"It can wait until tomorrow, William, it's dark out and far too long of a trip like this at night." In my defence, it was too far in the dark. Nearly a mile and a half with only the light of the half-moon—by foot, mind you.

"You have to give someone their birthday present on their birthday! Otherwise it's not a real birthday present!"

The matter was settled soon after. We would wait until morning and then go. I let him keep the picture so that he would know where to find it when he woke up. While tucking him in that night I told him that his mother loves him, and that I love him more than he could imagine.

"I love you too father. I love you too."

I kissed him goodnight, for the last time, and wandered off to bed.

While getting dressed the next morning, it occurred to me that I needed a present for Mary myself. She would have loved it if our twelve year old son showed up with a gift and I proudly strolled in empty handed. I took out from the closet a pair of black wool trousers and then dug until I found a dusty white cotton shirt. I pressed the shirt to my nose and held it there, closing my eyes. My wife had made it for me, giving me yet another reason to miss her. She would love to see me wear it again and that would be my gift to her. Although the shirt was old and had gone unworn for over a decade, it was much like me at that time—still young at heart.

After putting on the clothes, I decided to make us both an early breakfast so that after we ate, Will and I would have all morning to go to the cemetery. I cooked my son's egg sunny and snowed it with the tiniest flurry of pepper, before setting the plate down next to a basket of yesterday's bread on the table. After admiring my work for a few moments, I wandered down the hall and was surprised to find an empty bed upon entering Will's room. Nothing more was unusual. No note, no mess, nothing missing. Not thinking much more of it, I went to the cemetery, where I was sure I'd find him.

Upon arriving, I found not Will, but the picture instead. The present lay at the base of the grey stone, which read, *Mary Elizabeth Scott. 1887-1911. Soon we'll be eating rowan beneath the trees again.* I walked back knowing that Will would be home, probably in his room, waiting for a scolding. But I wasn't mad. How can a father be mad at his son for something as sweet as that?

When I arrived back the house was empty. Breakfast sat cold and uneaten. With each passing moment the terror in me grew. He should have been home by now. I went to notify the local sheriff. Will should have been home by that night, or the next day— but he wasn't.

I asked neighbors. I went to the center of town to tell everyone to spread word that Will had gone missing. Most of them asked me the same question. *Where was the last you saw of him?* In his bed, tucked in safe and sound, though full of minor resentment. No one had seen or heard anything. I spent countless hours at his favorite places, hoping to find him. I was helpless, knowing nothing can sometimes be worse than knowing the worst. I would sit down at the park in his favorite swing, hoping that at any moment Will would come dashing out of the nearby tree line and into my arms. I was afraid to look away because the moment I did would be the moment he would appear. I walked by the schoolyard each day, asking his friends the same questions until they began to resent me. In a way, I had already begun to resent them. They were here and Will wasn't.

Weeks went by and I stopped shaving. Strands of brown and grey hung from my face, usually hiding crumbs if I'd chosen to eat that day. Soon, I noticed that I was wearing the same clothes I'd chosen with such intimate care on that morning, which now seemed like an eternity ago. I figured maybe one day our conversation would be different, even if my shirt was the same.

"Anything, Sheriff?"

"I'm sorry, Scott." his usual response while shaking his head. I started to walk away. "And Scott," he bit his bottom lip, "You should probably change those clothes, 'cause I'm sure it'd do you a helluvah lotta good."

This was the extent of it, excluding that one day when he said that Will had probably run away. People stopped looking. And I started writing again.

I spend a lot of my time beneath the beech tree now. The window holds clean glass and the heavy wooden door is burnished. Home has changed in little ways. It's quieter and I no longer eat breakfast. I take pictures of the birds, this way I can write about them in the night. I send myriads of prayers up as well in the night. How can a man with such ephemeral happiness remain faithful? Maybe I owe that to the picture. Not a day goes by that I fail to look at it. In my sleep, I replay and am haunted by those last words: "I love you too father." The sincerity in his voice was unmistakable. So I hold on to this hope. A hope that wanes a little more each day. A hope that one day I will see my son again, or at the very least know what happened to him on the night of his mother's birthday. Hope that depresses me to drink and then a drink that inspires me to hope.

Epilogue: A Note From The Editor

William Scott has clung to his hope for the past eight-
een years since his son mysteriously vanished, producing some of the darkest, deepest poetry and stories of the twentieth century. Now age 54, Scott recently looked into an anthology of our poetry

that is set to be published next year, 1942. Halfway through reading the new volume, Scott made a startling discovery when he came across a poem written by him, that he could not recall writing. The title read: *I, Mary's Young Will.*

The Bistro

"They say he made it big time," one man said to another in a supermarket bistro.

"Who are they?"

"Whoever they are, that's who."

"I'm not so sure I believe them. That guy couldn't act for his life."

"It was for his life. Hollywood doesn't care if you eat or starve. He didn't have much of a choice. Apparently he got picked up at a bar. They needed extras, but some guy high up somewhere thought that he was pretty enough for some lines."

"I'll believe it when I see it," said the unsure man. He'd gone from wanting pizza for lunch to not being very hungry.

"How many people you suppose that happens to?"

"How many people does what happen to?"

"How many people you think make it like that after dropping it all and just going for it?"

The unsure man wasn't sure how to answer the question, so he ignored it. His friend was talking too much again. No one had made it big.

While the man who talked too much refilled his soda, the other man focused on counting the number of balloons that had gotten away and now rested as symbols of lost freedom against the high pale ceiling.

"You're right, ain't no way in hell he got picked up." The man returned with his drink.

"Fourteen."

"Huh?"

"Fourteen," the unsure man repeated louder, "balloons." He pointed at one with his finger.

The other, for a moment, was speechless.

"I suppose if he did make it, there'd be a movie coming out. And if he did make it and a movie was coming out, his name would be in the credits. I'd recognize his face if it weren't made up."

"Good luck with that."

"Luck with what?"

"Finding his name in the credits."

The man with a lot to say wasn't sure if his friend meant good luck because the guy probably didn't make it, or because it really would be lucky to find a specific person's name in the credits of an unknown movie—if the unknown movie even existed.

"How old do you think this place is?"

"Fifteen—maybe fifty, sixty years old. Older than either of us I'm sure."

"I'll bet it would be a good set for a movie. Good lighting," the man said, reaching for his soda.

"It's the high ceilings," the other answered, still looking up.

"What a story," the man bit his straw. "What a risk. Imagine the bravery or the stupidity in it, leaving it all for Hollywood. What a moron."

Impala

I saw a lady with no arms today.
Or maybe her arms were just pulled out of the sleeves of her jacket and gripped tightly to her body. Either way, it didn't matter. I still didn't see the impala coming.

So, because I want her to be armless, the lady had no arms. She was a middle-aged Korean woman. Or maybe she was Japanese. I remember her screaming when the car hit me. I had the little white man sign to cross, but you should always look. You should always look. And I usually do look, unless I'm in a crowd of people. When in a crowd of people, it's okay not to look, because if a car does run the light, someone else will take the worst of it. That's if you stay to the center of the crowd, like I usually do. But there was no crowd today. At least not before the impala.

A few years ago my uncle went a couple thousand miles to hunt impala in some desert in Africa. I can't wait to tell him that he didn't—or at least, I didn't—need to go all that way to see one. One came right up to me.

I noticed that they both had a black nose. The car itself was sand colored, not quite the orange of the animal, but close enough. It had one of those black bras on the front half of the hood to protect it from bugs or something. Now that I think about the animal more, they don't actually have a black nose. They more or less have black nostrils on a white face, but they still both had birds in common. In some of the pictures my uncle showed me of the impala he shot, there were birds perched on its body. Similarly, there was bird shit on the roof of the impala when the guy hit me. As I rolled up the hood and over the top, however, I didn't get the best look at it, so it may have been bird shit, or it may have been the white blotches of stars I saw when I opened my eyes in the air. Keeping them open was better than closing them for two reasons. First, to make sure that when I landed I didn't fall on my head or break my neck, and second, because when I closed my eyes the stars turned red, and red is a much more painful color to look at than white under such circumstances.

It felt good to fly, actually. For a brief moment, I was glad I got hit, because now I can say that I flew with the stars. I'm not embarrassed at the corniness of it. How many people can actually say they flew with stars? When I landed, everything went black. I faded in and out. When I was in, I heard the lady with no arms screaming. She was looking up at the sky and I didn't have the strength to tell her that I wasn't in the fucking air anymore. All of my energy went to imagining that my arms were gone. The pain made me wish that they were and I knew at least one of them was broken because I could feel the hot puddle of blood that had pooled under my left side. When I was out, I was dreaming of a cold, cold winter day. I was in the backyard at the house we lived in for the first three years I could remember as a kid. My brother and I were pushing each other on the tire swing which hung from the lowest branch on the tree in the center of the yard. I spun him around while he sat on top, straddling the rope, and then the branch broke and he fell to the ground. There was no snow, leaves, or grass to cushion him, but it was really windy and I began to shiver. My whole body started shaking until I shook from out of it back to into it and heard the screams again.

My favorite shirt was ruined. Out of everything I was unsure of, this was the one thing that I knew was true. Bob Marley's face was drawn in free hand pencil on the chest. The background was white, but his face was colored in three vertical stripes of green, yellow, and then red. The red was way darker than it should have been. I looked down and the face that was usually smiling was fitfully frowning. Underneath his smile and above his frown, the words "Wake Up and Live" were printed. I was able to read them twice over before I drifted out again.

They said that because of the construction happening on the corner, the ambulance had a hard time getting to me. Whenever the crane lifted another piece of concrete to the top of the new structure, the police had to stop traffic so that if the piece fell, it wouldn't crush anyone. I didn't mind waiting for the paramedics, though. It didn't feel like a long time to me. Despite what they tell me, I still think they got there pretty quickly, so I'm thankful for that.

I felt like I was flying again when they lifted the stretcher off the ground and for the first time since it happened, I was genuinely afraid. I wasn't ready for the unstable motion. I turned my head to vomit on the lady to my right and when I did, she said something to me about moving my neck.

I wasn't sure if she was talking to me or someone else, but I remember saying, "I'm sorry for your pants."

She stuck out her lips a little and told me to "shhhhh." She had a very pretty face and she reminded me of my mother as I looked up at her.

"And sorry for your shoes," I said before she told me to *shhhhh* again and I faded back out.

The first thing I thought about when I woke up was how stupid the pretty-faced lady was. You don't tell a person who is drifting in and out of consciousness to *shhhh*. You talk to them. You keep them awake and try to make them more aware of what's going on around them. What if the last sound I heard before I died was that pitiful sound she made at me? I was glad that I threw up on her. And I was a little bit pissed off at myself for apologizing for it.

I didn't even realize where I was, until I heard a familiar woman's voice—this one also to my right—scream, "My son! Justin, run quick and get your father, he's awake!"

This woman to my side was much more welcome to me than the last.

"My baby, oh my son," she said in a soothing tone.

"Mom?" I said, unsure if I was asking a question or calling to her as she stepped into my line of sight.

She kissed me on the forehead twice.

"Mom. My neck. I can't move my neck. Will I—" was all I could manage to say to her through deliberate breaths.

"Yes, you'll be able to walk again. Oh God, don't even ask that. I don't want to, I can't even…It's precautionary. They've stabilized it just to be safe."

My father came in next. He was followed close behind by Justin, who you met earlier on the swing.

"Good to see you up. Broken arm, broken leg, and a moderate concussion for you. Mild heart attacks for your mom and me."

Which arm? I asked myself, flexing both arms to see which one held more pain. The left, of course. It made perfect sense. The impala hit me from that side and the armless woman had been standing across the street slightly to the right.

I didn't have a headache then, not like I do now, anyway. I'd never really felt lucky to be alive like I did when I saw the people I care about the most crying for me. This appreciation for life, though welcomed, was fleeting. The nurse came in, asked us how we were doing, said that the doctor would be with us shortly, and then asked me if I needed to use the bathroom. I should have picked up on her saying use the bathroom instead of go to the bathroom. I said yes and wanted to die when I realized that this actually meant that I wasn't going to go to the bathroom at all.

Through more deliberate breaths, I asked my family to leave for a second. It shouldn't surprise you when a terrible day gets worse, but it always does. I hadn't wet the bed since I was five and yet, here I was.

When the nurse left, my family came back in. Justin was sporting a half smile that said, *when you get better you're going to hear about this.*

I was having trouble staying awake again. Almost ready to resign to sleep rather than fade out, I asked my dad if the guy in the car was alright.

"He's in the hospital here too, son. He was on his way here when he ran the red. His wife had just gone into labor."

"Is the baby?"

"You're fine, son. Everything is fine."

Something Subtle

"I will always love you," Daniel said.

Jackie pressed her husband's lips against her own, tasting her tears when their heads parted.

The doubts about their marriage had led them to this. One session with Dr. Browning, however, had left the two pitying anyone who disbelieved the efficacy of counseling. When he greeted the young couple, the doctor's eyes laid a calm reassurance on them. His confidence gave them faith.

"Please, do not feel ashamed," was the first thing he said. "Often people feel as if they have already failed by coming here."

Jackie wondered whether he began each greeting session like this. What a depressing line to have to say over and over each time you meet someone. He was right, though. Daniel, just six months removed from his wedding with his high school sweetheart, found this small feat of mind reading to be a remarkable and almost creepy establishment of credibility.

"I'm not sure that I know what else to do," the young lady spoke first, noticing the gentle thinness of Browning's face.

"Mind if I smoke?" the young man asked.

"It's your buck-fifty. Drink too if you'd like, so long as you share."

The doctor's light hearted response broke the tension for a moment and the wrinkles in Daniel's forehead dispersed like the unwrinkling of a bed sheet.

"This is a lovely office—"

"I'm a fan of sailboats."

Jackie shot a dirty look to her right, at her husband, as she readjusted herself on the black leather couch. The doctor paid no attention to the comment addressing the tiny schooner on his desk.

"It is a lovely office isn't it? Now where should we start?" Browning asked, raising his eyebrows slightly towards Jackie.

A fragile quiet settled on the room. It didn't surprise the doctor when the young woman spoke first.

"He's turned into a lazy asshole. That's the worst kind. You maybe wouldn't mind an asshole if he maybe got off of his ass and did something now and then. Would it kill you to do something when I ask? Would it kill you to do something on your own? How hard is it to wash a fucking dish? You're so difficult to love, Danny." She intended to cut him as much as possible in what she saw as her opening argument.

"You see, man, this is what I can't deal with. She never used to be such a bitch."

Browning wrote fluidly on his lined yellow notepad. As he did, silence overtook the three of them in the room again. He could tell when she turned away that the young woman was already crying. He reached for his end table, extended the tissue box to her, and she eagerly plucked it from his hand. It took only long enough for the doctor to cross his ankle over his thigh before she had composed herself enough to continue.

"He's a murderer. These are my dreams and here is Daniel," she said, stabbing the box of tissues in her left hand with the invisible knife she held in her right.

"Oh, don't give me that. I'm not the one holding you back, sweetheart. If you want to go to Europe, go right ahead. Better yet, go to hell."

Several minutes passed. No one spoke.

Jackie grew impatient waiting for an immediate apology. She threw the box at the floor, stood up, and kicked it. The box took flight with the energy form her foot, crashing hard into the sheetrock, which looked as if it were freshly painted. A brief feeling of embarrassment passed through her, but she decided that she didn't care, remembering that this doctor had undoubtedly seen much worse.

"Go ahead and throw it. I'm not the murderer, baby. You're the one who threw the knife."

"The knife?" one man asked the other.

"Yeah, man. She threw a steak knife at me. Twice." Daniel responded while holding his stare on his wife.

"It was two knives once, not one knife twice," she defended.

"And what provoked this?" Browning asked, willing to accept an answer from either one of them.

"He called me a whore."

"I said you were acting like a whore."

"It was a job interview, Danny. A job. You should look into getting one, you insecure fuck."

116

The couple had been living off of the money friends and relatives had given them for their wedding. Both families were well off, so the envelopes were enough to get them through until they both had full time jobs.

"This, believe it or not, is all good. It's not the people that come in here and yell at each other that I worry about. It's the ones that come and sit without saying much for most of the time that concern me. Now, I have to ask—and answer honestly, please—has it ever gotten more physical between the two of you?"

"I would never," said the young man with a hint of hurt in his eyes.

"And you?" the doctor asked, addressing the woman.

"No. I just feel so distant." She paused. "No. I feel that Danny is so distant."

Danny pulled at his cigarette after his wife's statement and looked up at the ceiling.

"I don't feel like I'm distant," he said, exhaling.

The man's disinterested look was disheartening, but he had begun to regret his harshness a moment before.

"You are too distant. We used to be so much closer," she said, turning her attention from one man to the other.

If eleven years of counseling had taught Browning one thing, it was that his first few minutes with a new couple were crucial. Everything about this brief period of time set up the way the rest of the relationships would go in therapy. Every word choice mattered.

"Do you really think that it is Danny that is distant, or could it be that you're both not as close as you used to be?" Browning offered.

Jackie was taken aback momentarily. This was not a matter of Danny being distant from her; rather, both of them were more distant from where they had once been with one another.

"I feel like he pays less attention to me now than when we were younger," she said.

"Would you agree?" asked the doctor.

"Of course not. Listen, when we were in school, from high school all on up through college, we always had other things going on. Our time together was limited. Whenever we were together, it was effortless. Now we live together, man. Sure, we're both out looking for jobs, but we're together a lot more."

"So you're saying that the two of you both valued your time together more when you saw less of each other," the doctor stated more so than asked.

"I mean, yeah. I would say it's like butter on bread. If you have the same amount of butter to cover a small and a large piece, you're obviously going to taste more butter when you bite the small piece. But even when you bite the big piece, the same amount of butter is still on the bread."

"So you both still have the same level of affection for one another, it's just spread thinner than before."

"Exactly, man"

Jackie didn't say anything. Instead, she pursed her lips and shrugged her shoulders.

"You said anything on our buck right?" was all she spoke as she slid off her boots.

Dr. Browning smiled compassionately and nodded as she lifted her heels onto the couch and wrapped her arms around her knees, pulling them in and making herself into a little ball.

"Ashtray," said the doctor with wide eyes. He pointed with his pen to the round glass object on the coffee table between them.

Daniel apologized while he flicked the grey soot and pressed what was left of the Camel into the slot designed to hold a live one. As he untied his shoes, it occurred to him that this was the first time he'd actually ever seen anyone use one of those slots before. He always figured they were more for show than actual use. When his toes were free, he leveraged himself up with his arms, crossed his legs like a pretzel, and slid them underneath his body.

To the casual observer, it would have looked like an innocent occurrence. But something truly remarkable had just happened. The subtlety of this subconscious act of bonding was quite romantic.

Inspired by this, while the two turned their heads fully toward each other and struggled to fight back laughter, the doctor leaned over with a repressed groan and untied his own shoes.

"Now that certainly is more comfortable," he said.

In all of his years, Dr. Browning had never taken his shoes off during a session before. It felt liberating. Every so often during his career he was blindsided by moments like this, where he was reminded that his patients helped him as much as he helped them.

The three sat contentedly for half a minute while the doctor wiggled his toes, coming to the conclusion that this was not only a nice office, but it had recently grown into quite a cozy one, too. Just then, the sound of raindrops could be heard on the windowpanes. If the three sitting in the room had been dogs, they all would have raised their ears simultaneously at the patter.

"So, you like sailboats, Daniel?"

"I do, but I've never been sailing before," he responded.

119

"It's quite an adventure." Browning was cuing up the homework assignment that ended each one of his sessions. "I want each of you for next week, to think of an adventure you'd like to go on. It can be anything. It doesn't even need to be realistic."

There was a lot of nodding going on around the room as they agreed upon the assignment and acknowledged that the same time next week worked for all three. Jackie and Daniel shook hands with the older man and walked out of the office, down the hall, and through the glass doors.

"You ready for this?" The man asked his wife as they stood underneath the overhang outside, gearing themselves up to run for the car. Jackie nodded and then smiled as Daniel's hand slid into hers and they began running down the steps and across the parking lot. They stopped just as they got to the trunk of their car, where the man whispered something into the woman's ear. They embraced and then parted, each making their way around a different side of the car.

Diego

Rumor has it that The Gopher hid the drug money in the hollow rocks down by the cove. Ramón knows better than to believe it, though. After seriously considering the hollows, he concluded that the rumor was started by The Gopher himself. Diego had earned the nickname because he had a gift for burying things—be it product or people. Ramón lived in the shadow of his brother's infamy for much of his life and although many people did not know that Diego even had an older brother, Ramón knew Diego better than anyone.

They used to climb the hollow rocks when they were kids. Both Diego, the thin boy with his long arms and Ramón, the shorter, plumper one with less leg strength, struggled to make their way up the rocks. Diego always justified his reasons for going first.

"I'm lighter and it's easier for you to push me up than me you. And you make such a good cushion when I fall, hermano."

There had been many times when they were unable to reach the hollows, but on their best days, and if it hadn't rained in a while, the boys could ascend far enough up to see the lighthouse over the treetops. The lighthouse was a big deal to the people of their town. It was built when the boys were five years old and with it came ships, imports, and commerce.

"Is it any greener?" Ramón would ask from the rocks below when Diego had made it up.

"Oh yes, much greener. You should come see it, brother."

Sometimes, Diego would leave Ramón where he was. He would go on describing the wonderful views. It was upsetting when this happened, but Ramón never responded with anger towards his little brother. Even though he was heavier and older, there was something in the way Diego carried himself that convinced Ramón that it was better to just let it go.

It would have been impossible to reach the hollows at thirty. So while the rest of the town searched down by the cove, Ramón took everything he knew about his dead brother into consideration.

The two room house which the small, broken family lived in had thin walls, holes in the roof, and occasional floods. It was always hot no matter the time of year and through most of the summer there was dampness in the air which made the walls sticky. It was under his bed in this miserable house where Ramón kept a shoe box. In it, protected from the water and air that the rest of the house endured, rested his most valuable treasures.

After lifting the lid with much care, Ramón moved the open box to his nose and breathed in. He attributed the wonderful smell to the book in the box. It was an American children's book written by Dr. Seuss. His mother would read this to him when he was sick or did not feel well and Ramón remembered wondering where it was that the cat in the hat was coming back from. Now, as he had learned when he grew older, he only had half of the cat's story. Also in this box were his ribbons for excellent attendance in grammar school and his ticket to Disney Land which his brother had made from orange construction paper and given to him for his birthday one year. After holding each of these fragile treasures for a moment, he laid them down on his bed and continued his search through the box. He ran his fingers along the green glass stem. It was cool, smooth, and while he smiled, Ramón closed his eyes and remembered the first time he'd used it.

"You're doing it wrong idiot," Diego said to Ramón. "You need to hold the flame closer to the stem."

His brother looked at him with hurt eyes. "You didn't tell me."

"I shouldn't have to. It's common sense."

"But—"

"But nada," Diego scolded. "Now breathe."

Ramón held the stem to his lips and inhaled slowly at first, then harder. He held his breath and exhaled when his brother began to laugh.

"Was that so hard? Now hand it here before the woman yells."

With his chest back and head tilted, Ramón extended his hand to Diego's. When their eyes locked and his brother gave a grinning nod, Ramón couldn't help but feel proud.

"Hijos, come down for dinner. Please don't make me tell you again."

His mother's call erased Ramón's pride. Guilt washed over him like the hose-water from the bucket she used to rinse them off with before they were allowed to enter the kitchen at the end of a long Saturday outside.

Ramón put the stem next to the book on the bed and wrapped his hands around the photo album he was looking for in the box. There was something indescribable that told him that Diego had buried the clue to where his fortune was hidden somewhere in the childhood that the two brothers shared. The album's cover had three sticker people on the front of it and the inside didn't contain more than a dozen pictures. He studied the people in the pictures well. He identified himself, his little brother, his mother, her sister, and their two cousins. He was hoping something would catch his eye in the pictures if he went through them slowly, but nothing did. So he flipped through them faster the second time and still found nothing. He had passed the picture four times in all by the time he recognized the lake behind the two sets of brothers in the ninth picture. This lake belonged to a house that his uncle had owned before he got sick and needed to sell it.

His mother with her two boys and his aunt and uncle with their two boys had met there once a year for two weeks every summer. Ramón recalled this as one of only two places where he had ever seen his brother truly happy. Having already ruled the first option out, the brother of the region's only drug lord packed a bag and set off for the second.

The place couldn't have looked more deserted when Ramón arrived. Several of the windows were boarded and those that still held glass were broken. The blackened, burnt hole in part of the roof indicated a fire that possibly started in the laundry room toward the back of the house. The stairs were broken and the weeds were advancing into the house. Ramón saw all of this as he stood outside what was once a place he looked forward to visiting very much.

Turning his head away from it and toward the lake, he saw Diego's ghost throwing stones across the black water down by the dock. Maybe the treasure was at the bottom of the lake. He strained his eyes and he saw a much older version of his brother struggling with a large, tightly locked chest. The older ghost was off balance as he carried it to the edge and then released it. The splash looked like a large cannon ball. Ramón blinked and all was gone.

He turned back to the house and imagined the ghost removing the floor boards precisely, with as much care as he did when he removed the top of the box beneath his bed. Ramón ran for the house with feet so light that they hardly touched the broken steps that led to the porch. He pressed forward on the knobless door, opening it with a creak, and stepped forward into the house for the first time in years. The smell of mold was in the air. There was dusty furniture sparsely thrown about the living room. Ramón heard a sound in the kitchen and made his way toward it with deliberate slowness. At the kitchen table he saw Diego, himself, and their uncle all sitting down for dinner. It was the last night either of them had spent in the lake house as children. The teenage boys were there, eating a roasted chicken that their aunt had left for their uncle and them.

"I'll tell you boys, if you ever go to New York City, it's like you're on a whole different planet. Every street is paved and there are cars and buses everywhere."

Diego could hardly stand it when his uncle spoke, but Ramón somewhat enjoyed the stories. They gave him both hope and sadness. The burnt food always tasted better while hearing of far off places.

"They have so many lights there. If you boys ever get to go there someday, you'll swear you're on a whole other planet."

You already said that, Diego thought to himself through gritted lips while he began to grind his teeth.

"There are stores of every kind up and down the streets. It's like that all over America. California. Boston. I've never been to either of those, but I can bet you it's like being on another planet."

Say it again, tío. I dare you, once more and I will. Diego glanced to the steak knife at the side of his plate. He was getting an ache in his temples as he increased the pressure on his teeth. His uncle went on talking about the way the currency looked, ending with the same words. Diego picked up the knife, held it so that the blade ran up his wrist, and threw a punch in the direction of his uncle's neck. The fist missed, but the jagged teeth of the blade bit the skin of the older man and bright red blood squirted out with a wet leaking sound. Diego laughed as his uncle held both hands to his throat desperately trying to hold the blood in.

This, of course, never happened. Ramón blinked again and shook his head from side to side once. There was a refrigerator along the left wall and a large wooden table nobly knelt on three legs. What looked like the remnants of chairs lay heaped in a pile like firewood at the center of the room.

Ramón spent two full days at the house. He dug holes in the ground outside so that the yard resembled a minefield. He tore the already dilapidated house apart even further. The treasure hunter was even sure he had found it when he beheld a wooden chest in a closet in one of the bedrooms; it was this that broke his spirit when he busted the lock and opened it to find only clothes. Unable to drain the lake, Ramón left the old house and went home. The wake was scheduled for the next day.

In the days before Diego swallowed the cyanide pills which took his life, he had made all the arrangements for his own wake, funereal, and burial. He would be laid out for a few hours the night before he was to be buried at sea. He oversaw the making of a beautiful custom coffin and had chartered a boat so that his mother and brother could release it into the water two miles offshore. The boys' mother cried uncontrollably when she found this out. In lieu of leaving a suicide note, Diego simply listed the events that were to take place after his body was found. In a town with no hope of escape, this ambitious young man had been able to find excitement, wealth, and fame. And there was a time not long ago when his mother pleaded with him to give it all up.

"No one will ever understand you as I do, mi hijo. And because of that, no one will ever be able to love you as I do. Please stop for my sake," she said to him with moist eyes.

But Diego was too good at what he did. His family accepted the nickname he'd earned because he was extraordinarily good at burying his feelings above all other things. Toward the end of his life, the two people closest to him could see that when The Gopher settled into his bed each night, he felt more and more tired. The last few years had aged him significantly.

"You can't take it with you. You cannot take it with you, mi amor."

The coffin was made of something that looked a lot like marble. It was dark blue, shiny, and resembled the way water itself looks when the sun hits it from a side angle. There was a smile on his brother's face as Ramón looked down into the casket.

"Your smile looks like diamonds, my brother, but I smile because I have lots of them," Diego had said a year ago, just before pulling open the bottom two dresser drawers in his room, revealing piles of diamonds that made Ramón's eyes sparkle. Although the drawers were empty the next time Ramón was able to sneak in and open them, he had beheld them with his own eyes. The treasure which many thought was mere myth, was very much real.

With no explanation from her dead son, their mother felt angry on the boat the next morning. Ramón had concluded that his brother had found too much excitement for one man to handle. He imagined an underlying anxiety that must have eaten Diego from the inside out until he finally found permanent peace. The priest made the sign of the cross over the coffin and two seamen helped the brother lift it and walk it over to the edge. The three men released their hands, and as they did, a faint clanking could be heard before the box hit the water. Ramón realized that it was not heavy simply because of the stone. There must have been loose rocks between the frame and the padded lining adding to the weight. And Ramón could only watch as his brother, the beautiful coffin, and The Gopher's fortune vanished to the bottom of the sea.

Shark Teeth

"There's nothing you can do about it! You'll never catch me," Dylan yelled as he raced away from the misshapen sandcastle. At two in the morning, there was no one there to stop us as we raced down the shoreline. Midnight sandcastles had become a weekly thing after school ended. He was fourteen and still very much immature, but that innocent playfulness was one of the most endearing things about him.

"You better hope I don't!" I tried my best to sound bold and angry, but laughter broke through. "What's the matter, afraid of a girl?"

As I got closer, he stumbled to the wet sand just before a wave broke, leaving a fine spray on his neck when the water collided with his bent knee.

"Gotcha," I panted as I grabbed his dirty blonde hair and pulled his head back until his face met mine, "now you're in trou—"

"Pick a hand," he said, holding up two closed fists.

I picked the one on the right. When his fingers flattened, there rested a v-shaped tooth the size of a bottle cap softly in his palm. I slowly reached down to touch it and his fingers closed on mine.

"Pick another hand," he raised his left fist slightly. I tapped it and it opened like a clam revealing a pearl, proudly displaying a slightly smaller tooth. On pure reaction I went to touch this one, too, momentarily unaware of the fate my other hand had just recently met. My mouth opened to say something, but his smile froze my tongue. "I fell on purpose."

Wisdom is bound to come with age. Having graduated high school this past spring, I can almost feel the seeds of it which took root in me long ago growing taller by the day. I'm only going to community college, so while a part of me feels like I'm growing up and moving on, I'm really not going anywhere. As I look out at the ocean through my window, I imagine what it would be like to leave this home I've grown so tired of since Dylan was taken away from me.

I hadn't met Dylan until I was fifteen. When my parents moved my brother and I from our home in Baltimore down to Virginia Beach, Dylan was one of the first friends I'd made. Well, actually, he was one of the first friends my little brother, Scott, had made. Both of them were fourteen and going into their first year of high school. They had math together and my brother, being the lazy kid that he was, asked Dylan for last night's answers on just the second day of class. He agreed under the condition that he would get to come over to our house for dinner that night. Scott didn't think long on it, the trade was made and a friendship was formed. When he came to the table to eat and said hello to me for the first time, I didn't see his lips move. His grey eyes did all the talking. I'd never seen a boy our age with grey eyes before. They saw my curious concern and with a concern of their own they said, *come to me. Watch me watch you and when no one else is watching, I have dangerous things to show you.*

Dylan came over for dinner a lot because his parents never got along. He'd confided in me that he couldn't remember a time when they weren't fighting over something. They were in the process of going through a messy, violent divorce, and the judge overseeing the case determined their house to be an inhospitable environment for a young boy. The closest family he had was an aunt and an uncle on his mother's side, but they lived in Colorado. It was predetermined before they even told him that he was going to be moved by the end of the summer so that he could start the school year fresh.

I remember him crying when he told me. We'd grown so close over the past year and Scott had long ago accepted the fact that Dylan came over more and more to see me rather than him. I remember crying myself, for Dylan, when he told me that he told the caseworker he'd rather stay here with his divorcing parents and at least have his friends than go live alone with strangers. And I remember that I actually convinced my Dad to say that it would be okay for Dylan to stay with us for a little while until his parents got everything settled.

Thinking back, I like to indulge myself every so often in imagining how different the end of my childhood would have been if the court would have allowed Dylan to stay at our house. Our home was small back then, like most of the houses close enough to see the shore from, but it's only getting smaller as Scott and I get bigger. We fight over the bathroom constantly and we nearly come to blows when we can hear each other's music coming through the thin wall which separates my room from his on the second floor. Another person would have meant less space and even more fights than there are now, but it wouldn't matter. The half empty feeling I go through life with would feel as full as our house should be.

The summer he got taken, it was no secret that the end of the road wasn't meant to be the end of the road. Budget cuts had driven the workers away and when they left, they left a treeless dent in the forest. It had been a popular hangout the previous summer, but since then it had been mostly forgotten by all other kids. The sign at the beginning of the street may have read Dead End, but the cleared trees and flattened ground beyond where the gravel stopped offered hope. One night, Dylan and I ignored the sign's warning and walked down the road alone.

"Nice sandals," he said. "They're new."

The way he noticed the little things made me blush.

"Your hands are cold, you should have worn a jacket," I said.

"Your feet look cold, you should have worn socks."

When we got to the end of the road, we kept going until we got to a tree with roots that branched out thick from the base like the arms of a chair. While we talked, we traded my jacket for his socks, and neither one of us was cold after that.

"That's a raccoon," he stated proudly at the rustling of leaves, "It's too big to be a squirrel."

A moment passed, wings flapped, and we heard a *caw*.

"That's a night hawk," I said, "and I think we're both smart enough to get crickets." I didn't move my head from his shoulder, but I could feel him smiling.

It was surprising how many different animals you could hear wide awake in the middle of the night and we continued to take turns naming them until we began to repeat. He stood up first as we got ready to leave and when he pulled me to my feet I felt the shaky unpaved ground through his socks. I leaned on him for balance, he was slightly taller, and when I looked up I could see the lone streetlamp behind me reflected back twice in his eyes. That's the moment when I realized I believed in God. Nothing man-made could have ever been so perfect.

It was a helpless feeling. He was afraid of the loneliness that was waiting for him at his new home and I was afraid of the emptiness that would later come to consume his old one. When the day came on which I had to swallow the daydreams I'd grown used to dreaming, we didn't have much time to say goodbye. His aunt and uncle had arrived promptly. For weeks, part of me wished that their plane would melt into the sun or that an earthquake would swallow their car on their way to Virginia. This longing for some kind of miracle only grew more intense as that day grew nearer. These were the lucky people that were taking my best friend away. These were the people who would get to watch him grow into the great man that I knew he would become. And I hated them for it.

We promised to stay in touch online and on the phone. After all, this was only supposed to be temporary, and the thought of him returning has been my teddy bear for many nights since. My parents helped bring his bags down from our porch. He spent his last night home with my family gathered around a campfire and the way the orange glow tanned his skin mesmerized me. As far as I know, his parents never even said goodbye. As the adults exchanged meaningless conversation, Dylan and I exchanged a more meaningful *this isn't goodbye forever.*

When we went to hug I began to cry. He pulled me close and for a moment our bodies felt hollow. Our arms were squeezed tightly and felt light, like an intense case of pins and needles. I hoped that if I kept my eyes closed long enough, everyone would just disappear when I opened them. He whispered in my ear, *check your pocket after I leave.* I kept my eyes closed tight, but when I opened them, he was the one who disappeared instead.

I tried my best to bond with my little brother the first month without Dylan. I like to think that he also tried his best to understand how I was feeling, but he just didn't get it.

"I don't get this show," Scott said as we watched TV together on a Saturday morning. Even though we were teenagers, we still watched cartoons. "This kid has fairy godparents and he's always so miserable."

"He has to be miserable, otherwise there wouldn't be any show." We both had a strong argument. I couldn't help but think that Timmy Turner was misusing his fairy godparents. My mind left the Nickelodeon program and drifted off to a world where I had magic fairies to grant anything I wished. It wasn't hard to think of a wish; one would be all I needed and then the godparents were free to go to another person in need. The only debate was whether to wish for Dylan to come back or to never have left at all. If he never left, neither of us would have ever had to be sad about being apart, but at the same time I knew that us being apart only made me care for him more. I never got to decide which I would ask for though.

"It's unhealthy for her," I heard my dad say from the breakfast table. He didn't even make an effort to lower his voice. "I had a feeling that this would happen. I'm taking her phone away."

"Calm down, Frank. It's only a progress report." My mom tried her best to talk him down, but my father had already pushed his chair away from the table. He cast a bald headed shadow on the hardwood floor before he passed through the doorway that separated the kitchen from the living room.

The vibration of his footsteps in the floor boards had intimidated my brother and I for as long as we could remember. Despite this, however, there was always a warm wrinkle of concern stapled to his forehead and he was nice enough to dismiss Scott from the room before he spoke to me. "Tell me what the problem is, Katherine."

I don't know why he had such a difficult time seeing that I wasn't ready to get over Dylan so soon and I probably never will be. Hesitating at first and then stuttering through words only made me look guilty for what should have been considered an innocent crime.

"This is outrageous. Unnecessary. Unacceptable."

With that he took the phone away from me and grounded me for a month. I didn't put up much of a protest, I just went to my room and stared out the window. I think my parents felt a mix of pity for me and shame for themselves. They realized that I was trying so desperately to hold on to someone they had already deemed gone, and they felt shame because they didn't realize I missed him as much as my spiraling grades said that I did.

A half hour later, the floor started to vibrate familiarly before I felt my father standing outside my door. He knocked twice and then twisted the knob before I offered a response. "I'm sorry that you feel so sad. I wish there were a way for me to bring him back for you. I wish there were a way for me to pull you out of this." He handed me my phone. "You're still grounded."

I probably owed my mother a thank you for his fast change of mind. I hadn't lost my phone for long, but what I had lost was some of the security I felt when I used it. I thought of how much comfort his voice brought me and realized how much worse things would be if the only way I could hear it was through memories.

After he left, I felt the paper in my pocket as I watched the car pull away. I waited until I got back to my room so that I could safely read it:

Katie, when you get the chance, please go to our arm tree at the end of the road.

I spent the better part of that afternoon sitting on the curb outside of Dylan's house when I heard a voice I recognized as his dad's ask,

"Who the fuck are you?"

I'd only met his parents once before and it didn't surprise me that he didn't remember me. I didn't say anything back to him, I just got up and left, thinking to myself that it was amazing they didn't fuck Dylan up by being such terrible people. I should have blamed them for him getting taken away, but I was too overwhelmed to think on that thought long.

I went that night to the tree at the end of the Dead End road and bent down to trace our freshly carved names with my fingertips. A warmth rushed over me as the bark split my skin, but I didn't care. It was the warm sensation of security and the memory of traded white socks.

At the base of the tree there was a folded piece of paper with a stick through it in the ground. I removed the stick and opened it:

I bet you hear the crickets and the hawks and the raccoons. But listen.
Now dig... I hear sharks.

I found the hole in the dirt where the stick had been stuck and began to dig around it. The soil was loose and it wasn't before long that I was holding two small v-shaped teeth, one slightly larger than the other.

I never like to think about the first few conversations Dylan and I shared after he was taken, but thinking about them makes me realize that my problems are never as bad as they seem. Having to move across the country to live with relatives you don't know can be depressing enough, but being picked on for being different can really hurt a kid, no matter what age. Dylan told me how the first few days of school had left him branded with the nickname, "the new kid." They laughed at his accent and the surfer hair he wore that had no business being so far away from the ocean. A warm heart doesn't stand a chance secluded in the unforgiving Rockies, surrounded by cold faces. He said he felt distant, like he was being punished for the crimes his parents had committed against one another long ago.

What was even worse was that he was being punished for all the little crimes he was committing himself, no matter how insignificant. His aunt began by pulling his hair or ear without warning when he forgot to take out the trash. His uncle put him to work around the big yards when he wasn't at school. They thought that Dylan owed them something. They thought they had the right to hit him when he didn't do a job perfectly or when he avoided coming home after school. He sent me pictures of the bruises once, but never again after I freaked out. These people didn't have the right to do that to a young man who didn't even belong to them. There was nothing either of us could do. My heart broke for him. He was suffering, a prisoner in his own home.

When I told my parents what was happening in Colorado, they chalked my concern up to exaggeration and a cry for attention.

"Kate, honey, I'm sure nothing is ever as bad as it seems." She was wrong. "Your father and I have been talking and if you stay focused at school and help out around the house, we're willing to let you go visit him for a week. Or better yet, we'll fly him back here."

My heart skipped at the idea. I stayed focused and even made the honor roll for the first time in my life and I was more than eager to help out at home. When I re-approached my parents on the subject a few months later, though, they said that it was no longer an option. I felt betrayed. I wondered if they had ever actually intended to fly Dylan back or allow me to visit at all. The whole thing had clearly been a white lie of love to pick my spirits up. That's what I thought at least, until I brought the subject up to Dylan and he said that his aunt and uncle pretended not to know who my parents where when they called.

"The seagulls miss you more than I do." I joked to him. We used to feed them pizza crust from the benches by the streets where the beach began.